Deep Level

Richard E Rock

www.darkstroke.com

Discover us online:
www.darkstroke.com

Join us on instagram:
www.instagram.com/darkstrokebooks/

Include **#darkstroke** in a photo of yourself
holding this book on Instagram and
something nice will happen.

For Christine and Zeb.

Acknowledgements

The following people all played an invaluable part in helping this book to see the light of day:

Everyone at The Wave and Swansea Sound for giving me My Big Break as a writer.

My good friends in the Swansea and District Writers Circle for their advice, encouragement and enthusiasm.

Laurence and Stephanie Patterson at darkstroke for their belief in me and my work.

And finally, my parents, for raising me in a home filled with books, music and creative energy.

I owe them all my deepest thanks.

About the Author

By day, Richard E. Rock works as a commercial scriptwriter for radio and contributes ideas to a popular British comic for grown-ups. But by night…he writes horror.

He was inspired to do this after experiencing a series of particularly ferocious nightmares. After waking up and realising that he could turn these into utterly horrible stories, he started deliberately inducing them.

Based in Wales, he lives with his girlfriend and their cat. If you're looking for him, you'll probably find him wedged up against the barrier at a heavy metal gig, for that is his natural habitat.

Deep Level

BOOK ONE:

GROUND LEVEL

Chapter One

It began early one morning, and ended later that same day. It was a November morning, cold and dark, and the wind carried a touch of the Arctic. The buildings loomed black and erect like tombstones against the sky, which was a deep cosmic-blue and star-sprinkled.

The lifelessness of Gunnersbury Lane was broken by the huffing and puffing of a lone woman, engaged in a peculiar sort of non-run; arms moving rapidly, legs not so much.

Ffion was late, as usual. *You're like a bloody train*, her friends would say. *You'll be late for your own funeral.* She wondered what cheeky remarks were in store in the cafe where two of them were waiting.

It was the shock of bright red hair through the window that first snared Syeeda's gaze. "Aha! Head's up," she said, as a rosy-cheeked Ffion slinked in through the door. "The human matchstick has finally arrived!"

"What was it today then?" asked Rosalind, looking back over her shoulder. "Leaves on the line? Wrong kind of snow?"

"Shuddup," said Ffion with a sheepish grin.

The windows were streaked with condensation as the warm air inside collided with the cold morning frost without. The place smelled of tea and beans.

"Alright, Jase?" Ffion asked the man in the apron behind the counter. "How about a cuppa then? I'm bloody knobbled."

"ANYTHING ELSE, LOVE?" boomed Jason. He did not do quiet.

Ffion looked back at her friends. Rosalind had a bacon buttie in front of her and Syeeda was getting stuck into a plate of beans on toast. No butter. She felt a pang in her belly.

"Have whatever you want, Fee," said Rosalind. "It's on me."

"Full English, please, Jase."

"THAT'S MY GIRL!" Jason bellowed. From behind his steamed-up glasses he ogled Ffion up and down with longing eyes. He had nursed a thing for her since she'd arrived in this particular corner of London (with small child in tow) from the south Wales town where she'd grown up. Unfortunately for him, she had relocated to be with her boyfriend. That was two years and another baby ago.

"HAVE A SEAT THEN, MY DARLING, AND I'LL BRING IT OVER TO YOU!" He hauled his tall, gangly frame off to the kitchen where he proceeded to yell something at an understrapper.

Ffion pulled up a chair and, as she sat down, gave Rosalind's hand a little squeeze. "Thanks, Roz," she said.

"That's alright," replied Rosalind. "God knows how long we're going to be down there for, so you've got to get some fuel in you."

"Well, I hope it's not going to be too long. Greg's mam's coming over later and she said she'd treat us to a Harvester."

"Can I come?" asked Syeeda.

"No. Bugger off," chuckled Ffion.

"Charming."

"So what's the German for breakfast?" Rosalind asked Syeeda.

"Frühstuck."

"And beans on toast?"

"Um. Bean is Bohne, so beans must be Bohnen. I don't know what toast is but bread is Brot."

"Still at it then?" said Ffion.

"You're certainly starting to sound more German," said Rosalind.

"Yeah. I sussed out that in Germany they say their R's in the back of the throat."

It was a few weeks spent hiking in the Stubai Alps in Austria with her sister the previous summer that had inspired

Syeeda to start learning the lingo. She already spoke two languages and she liked the idea of being truly multilingual.

"So are you still planning on going back?"

"Yeah. We're looking at maybe next summer."

"And how is Jas?"

"Great, actually. Up to her eyes in work but that's how she likes it."

As Syeeda was talking, Ffion was fishing her mobile phone out of her bag. She placed it on the table in front of her and swiped the screen. Rosalind cleared her throat. Ffion looked up to see Rosalind's eyes dart down to the phone and then back up to meet hers.

"Oh yeah. Sorry. Forgot." Ffion put her phone back in her bag.

"She did that to me too." Syeeda sighed.

Rosalind ran a hand through her short, greying hair. "Have I told you my theory about why the zombie is the bogeyman for the modern age?" she asked, addressing both of her friends.

"And this has what to do with mobiles?" asked Syeeda with an arched eyebrow.

"You'll see." Rosalind smirked. "In America in the fifties, it was all flying saucers and aliens. That's because their biggest fear at that time was the threat of Soviet invasion. So the whole flying saucers thing was a metaphor for invasion. In the eighties it was all body-horror movies, like The Thing and The Fly, because of AIDS. The corruption of the body. Go back about fifteen years or so and that's when the so-called torture-porn movies started coming out, because America was stomping across the Middle East renditioning people and waterboarding them."

Ffion was transfixed. Where was Roz going with all this?

"In Japan it was Godzilla and other assorted giant mutated monsters, because of the fear of radiation after the atomic bombs. But the bogeyman for today is the zombie. Everywhere you look, there's zombies; Walking Dead, World War Z, Pride and Prejudice and Zombies. You can go and have zombie experiences where actors in make-up will chase you around, for god's sake. And why? Because of these."

She pulled her mobile phone out of her pocket and held it up.

Ffion and Syeeda looked at each other blankly."Okaaay," Syeeda eventually said. She sounded unconvinced.

"Yep. Every single day, everywhere you go, all you see are people plodding along, stupefied, phones in hand, not looking where they're going, mouths hanging open, only half aware. And what do they all look like?"

"Zombies," said Syeeda and Ffion in unison.

Smugly, Rosalind slipped her mobile back into her pocket.

"But *you've* got a mobile." Ffion couldn't help but point out.

"Yes, but mine's not a smartphone," replied Rosalind. "It's not internet-enabled, and I certainly don't plod around staring at it when my attention should be on what I'm doing. Not that there's going to be much of a signal where we're going today."

"Or any signal at all, for that matter," added Ffion.

"I would literally die without my phone," Syeeda stated firmly.

It was at moments like this that Rosalind usually called Syeeda out on her use of the word'literally', but it was still early and right now she simply couldn't be bothered.

"I have to say," said Ffion to Rosalind, "I never had you down as the type to go poking around in old tunnels full of rats. I thought you were too posh for all that."

"Oh, thanks a bunch!" Rosalind gasped, genuinely offended. "Posh indeed!"

Syeeda laughed. Basically, Ffion thought that anyone who had a degree was posh.

"And what about you, Syd?" asked Ffion. "I thought you were supposed to be out on a date today."

"Well, I was," Syeeda replied with a curl of the lip, "but I called it off. To be honest, I'd rather be hanging out with you guys, even if it is in some grotty old subway."

"Aw, bless you," said Rosalind.

"Yeah, cheers, Syd." Ffion smiled. "So, how's work

going?"

"S'alright," Syeeda replied with a lazy shrug. "Been on wars this week."

"What are wars?" Ffion asked.

"Work available reports."

"Some of the work jargon you come out with absolutely blows my mind," said Rosalind. "My favourite one is the warm hand-off."

"What the hell's a warm hand-off?" Ffion spluttered.

"Transferring a live call to a specialist," replied Syeeda.

Rosalind shook her head. "I can't get over the fact that instead of just calling it 'transferring a call to a specialist', they called it a 'warm hand-off'. Jesus."

"I think it's amazing, I do." Ffion beamed. "Any jobs going?"

"Back-end access is another one," Syeeda continued, ignoring Ffion's question. "You'll often hear someone asking someone else if they have back-end access."

"So what does that one mean?" laughed Rosalind.

"If you have database access."

"Working in your place sounds like a Carry On film."

"A what?" Syeeda asked.

"Never mind."

"Have you got any more stories for me to read then, Syd, is it or what?" asked Ffion.

In her spare time, Syeeda wrote and illustrated short stories, which she circulated amongst her friends before putting them into a box and then forgetting about them. Ffion was her biggest fan.

"Almost. I'm working on one now about the boy who invented the spitball."

Ffion's face lit up. "The boy who invented the spitball? Brilliant. I don't know how you come up with this stuff. What's it called?"

"Charles Lippincott Ball."

"You're wasted in the civil service, Syd," said Rosalind. "You should be a writer."

Syeeda said nothing.

"How's work with you then, Fee?" asked Rosalind, picking up the slack of the conversation.

"You won't believe what happened yesterday," she scowled. "Some woman came in with her two kids, bought them tickets and some popcorn and stuff and then left them there to watch a film. When she came back later there was no sign of them – they'd buggered off early – and she went ballistic. Started blaming us. Went up the wall, mun!"

"So she was using the cinema as a cheap babysitter, basically," said Rosalind.

"Not that bloody cheap, but yeah. She was really kicking off, so we had to call security on her."

"How old were they?"

"Security?"

"No. The kids. Did she find them?"

"About ten or twelve, I reckon. And I dunno. Security told her if she didn't calm down, they'd call the police on her and she'd probably get nicked for neglect as well as threatening behaviour or whatever."

"What film was it?" asked Syeeda.

"Does that really matter?" Rosalind asked with a wry smile.

"It matters to me."

"Last Jedi," said Ffion.

Syeeda rolled her eyes. "No wonder they left early."

"Mmm," Ffion agreed.

"HERE YOU GO, MY PRECIOUS!" boomed Jason as he placed a steaming-hot full English breakfast in front of Ffion. "I'VE THROWN A COUPLE OF BLACK PUDDINGS ON THERE AS WELL FOR YOU! ON THE 'OUSE!"

"Aw, cheers, Jase," said Ffion, giving him a little wink. "You're a star, you are." She was well aware of his feelings for her and could have played him like an Xbox, but she wasn't that kind of person.

She had started dating her first husband at the age of twenty, back in 2008. Or, as Fionn was someone who measured time by movies, when Iron Man, Kung Fu Panda and Twilight were on release. They were married four years after that, in 2012 (The Avengers, Skyfall), and welcomed their first and only child together, Iwan, a year later (Despicable Me 2, Frozen). In 2014 (Guardians of the Galaxy, Maleficent) Ffion discovered that her husband was "doing the dirty" on her. The following year (The Force Awakens, Minions) she left her boy with her mam for a week and went on holiday with her Carmarthen friends to Portugal and met her current boyfriend, Greg. Actually, she did more than just meet him, and in 2016 (Rogue One, Deadpool) she gave birth to her second son, Geraint. By this time, she had jacked in her job in Carmarthen and joined Greg in Acton so that they could all be a family together, and so far, so good.

"So," she said, "what time's Rich picking us up?"

***

He had hoped to be up and out before his wife and daughter woke up, but alas it was not to be. As he (as silently as possible) began to eat his breakfast and peruse the morning's news on his laptop, his daughter Mimi's laser-attuned hearing detected life downstairs, and so she sprang out of bed to indulge in one of her favourite pastimes: watching her father eat.

Rich's spirits plummeted when, clad in her favourite Minions pyjamas, Mimi slid in through the door and delicately rested her chin on the edge of the dining table, grinning all the while.

"What are you doing, Mimi?"

"Watching you eat, daddy."

"Go and put the TV on, darling," he said.

"No." She was still grinning.

"Go and watch TV, Mimi, please." It was worth another shot.

"No."

"Why don't you go and get a colouring book or something?"

"No. I want to watch you eat."

It was those rare, quiet moments that Rich treasured most,

11

when he could eat breakfast and read the news or do the crossword in peace, but they had started to become increasingly rare, and right now every mouthful was torture.

"Daddy?"

"Yes, Mimi?"

"I love you."

Oh, god! he thought."Thank you, Mimi."

"Do you love me?"

"Of course I do."

Throughout this exchange, Rich's expression floated somewhere between distraction and complete disinterest. He had a face that naturally gave nothing away. Had he ever decided to take up poker he'd have been champ. It was this quality that, for most people at least, made him so hard to read. Ironic, really, as he made his living in the book trade.

That mask was hiding a man who, no matter where he was, always felt as if he didn't belong. It was his default setting, it seemed to him.As if he had been placed on Earth to fulfil the role of an observer as opposed to a participator. He was not the sort of person who could lose themselves in the moment, get carried away, get caught up. People who could become one with the crowd and lose their minds at a football match or a rock concert were an enigma to him. How did they do it? Was it something they had that he didn't or was it the other way around?

When Marie, his girlfriend since college, had broken with tradition and asked him to marry her (she knew that she would be in for a very long wait otherwise), he had said yes. Not because he loved her, but because he couldn't be entirely sure that he didn't. Yes, he had feelings for her and didn't want to lct hcr down, but did that qualify as love?

And when she had introduced the subject of starting a family, he had looked into her eyes and realised that this was the one thing that she wanted more than anything else, so once again he had said yes. He had done this to make her happy. Did this also qualify as love? Possibly.

When he had told the people around him that his wife was expecting, they had said, 'Wow! Congratulations, mate!

That's brilliant news!' And they had shaken his hand and hugged him and slapped him on the back. 'I'm made up for you, fella! That's brilliant!'

This had made him feel good. It had made him feel warm and wanted. It was a nice feeling. Throughout Marie's pregnancy he had been kind and attentive and patient and understanding. And he had been happy. He had enjoyed being a part of that small, growing family.

And people had said to him, 'Just wait till you're holding that baby in your arms for the first time. There isn't a feeling in the world like it. You'll fall instantly in love with them and every fibre in your being will suddenly find itself with one sole purpose, to protect that little baby no matter what. It's incredible'.

The day had come earlier than expected, and Rich, having just cycled frantically from his bookshop to the hospital, had found himself standing in a delivery room holding a tiny, purple, crying creature and staring down into its dark, desperate eyes.

"It's a girl," Marie had said. Tearful, blissful Marie.

"A girl," Rich had repeated. And so, he had stood there patiently waiting for the tidal wave of emotion to kick in, for the gushing sensation of love, for the eruption of protective, paternal instinct. But nothing came.

After finding himself a father at the age of twenty-five, Rich did not work less in order to spend more time with his family, he worked more. He had started at the bookshop as a part-timer, eventually becoming full-time. He had put in extra hours 'sweating the small stuff', learning the intricacies of the ordering system, negotiating the labyrinth of the staff rota, the complexities of the payroll, employee rights and retail law, pricing, finances. And thanks to his unfeeling, logical mind and his unswerving dedication to duty he had been promoted to assistant manager – and then eventually to manager. He liked this new role. It meant that he could spend even less time at home. But even then, it was too much, so he had found himself a hobby.

Rich had stumbled upon the joys of urban exploration: the

discovery and recording of the forgotten and abandoned buildings, tunnels and recesses that the rest of humanity walked past, over or around every day without ever noticing.

To find himself standing completely alone in a mysterious, hidden place where, quite possibly, no other human being had set foot in over a century, thrilled him. Yes, it actually provoked feelings in him, something that not even the birth of a daughter had achieved. In urban exploration he had at last found his thing, his passion, his calling. What a shame that he had found it too late, after he had said yes...twice.

The more time he spent in cavernous bunkers underground, or in derelict asylums, the less interest he had in his home life, his marriage, and his job. This was all he wanted to do. He wanted to discover, to explore and to share. And luckily, the technologies of the age allowed him to do just that, along with providing him with the potential means of his escape.

He resolved to set his logical mind into action once again. He would sweat the small stuff, he would crunch the numbers and he would do the homework, and eventually he would find the formula for monetising his hobby.

He calculated how many Facebook, Instagram, YouTube and Twitter followers he would need in order to be able to capitalise on the available revenue streams (advertising, sponsorship) that inevitably followed. With that money he would be able to afford a good standard of living (even in London!) whilst providing for his ex-wife and child – and he would be free!

But in order to win over that many followers, he would have to come up with something special. It would involve a lot of research, and for this he would require help in accessing and navigating the city archives. But that was okay. He had a friend in that department.

***

"Wait till I tell you what happened to *me* in work yesterday," said Rosalind.

"Whassat, then?" asked Ffion.

"You're not going to believe this, but I was in the locker room, and bent down to get something out of my locker, and I farted..."

"Oh my days," squealed Syeeda. "You farted!"

Jason's head cocked in their direction.

"Shush!" Rosalind hissed. They all leaned in close and she continued. "So I farted – loudly – and everyone looked over and, for a split-second, I was just standing there, frozen, wishing the ground would open up and swallow me whole, and – get this – a young man who works with us called Kevin said he did it. He took the blame for me."

"You're kidding!" gasped Syeeda.

"Yeah. He said, 'Oops, sorry everyone. It just slipped out'."

"Oh, love him," Ffion gushed.

"Hang on," said Rosalind, "this gets better. So there's a girl who's just started working with us called Katie – newly qualified archivist, very pretty – and Kevin's absolutely crazy about her. I mean genuinely besotted with her, but she doesn't know it. He hasn't got the courage to ask her out. He's a bit shy like that. Anyway, she was there when it happened and afterwards she came up to me and she said: 'I can't believe what Kevin did earlier. I was thinking of asking him out, but he can forget it. I'm not going to date someone who farts in public. That's disgusting'. And off she flaunts."

"So did you tell her it was you who done it?" asked Ffion.

"Absolutely not!"

"Roz, mun! You've got to tell her! That poor boy!"

"Well, I'll think about it," Rosalind shrugged, in a manner that implied that she was not going to think about it at all. She caught sight of the reflection of herself in the cafe window. Outside all was still dark, so it was much like looking in a mirror. She ran a hand through her short, greying hair and contemplated herself. She liked what she saw.

To a young brown girl newly arrived from Sierra Leone, London had been a bewildering and even frightening place. It was so huge! How did anyone ever learn to find their way

15

around? But she could only be held prisoner by the feelings of loneliness and hesitation for so long, however, and eventually it was music that had set her free.

Thanks to her ability to moonstomp like a pro and her made-ya-look resemblance to Pauline Black of The Selector, she had found her place – her tribe – amongst the rude boys and rude girls of the ska scene.

Rosalind had arrived. And it was with her help that Rich had begun to build a three-dimensional map of the world beneath London. It had been a mammoth task, far bigger and more complicated than he could have conceived. But that was okay. He liked a challenge.

What lies beneath? In the case of old London town, a great deal indeed. Governments, private enterprises and wealthy individuals had been digging down into the London soil for over a hundred and fifty years, and as well as the openly documented things like subway systems, sewers and service tunnels, there were also hundreds of other, far more opaque building projects waiting to be unearthed; fallout shelters, billionaires' mega-basements, crypts and catacombs. In a grimmer vein there were also undocumented burial sites and plague pits.

He was looking for something, something new and exciting and unexplored, but at this point he had no idea what. As his three-dimensional map developed, something occurred to him: it wasn't data that he should be looking for, but the lack of it. There were holes in the map, black holes, empty spaces, and no amount of research could fill them. Of course, it was always possible that no one had ever tunnelled out these spaces. But then, it was equally possible that they *had* been dug out and developed, but in secret. He had become gripped with a fuzzy kind of excitement. He was on to something. He just knew it.

"Will you watch Minions with me?" Mimi asked, jolting Rich from his reverie. *For the four-hundredth time this week*, he added in his mind.

"Pleeeeaaaase!"

"Not right now, sweetheart. Daddy's got to finish his

breakfast and then he's got to go out." He glanced down at the time in the corner of the laptop screen and his heart skipped. If his wife didn't get up soon, he would be stuck with Mimi until she did, and he had to leave in approximately fifteen minutes. Rich was not the sort of person who liked having to work with approximates, but as a parent, there was no choice.

Going upstairs and waking his wife up on her day off was absolutely NOT an option. Things were getting desperate. He didn't want to resort to sneakily suggesting to Mimi that perhaps *she* could go upstairs and wake mummy up, but he might have to. But then, to his glorious relief, he heard noises above him; footsteps, a yawn, more footsteps, the toilet flushing, the shower starting. He sighed deeply as his pulse began to ease.

"Mimi. Mummy's awake."

"Hooray!" cried the child as she ran out of the room.

This was his chance. In order to ease his escape, he had planned ahead and loaded up his car the night before. In the boot was a video camera (a Sony Handycam FDR-AX100 4K Camcorder, ideal for filming in low-light conditions), a set of night-vision goggles (an AN/PVS-14, as used by the SAS, no less!), three head torches for the girls (the cheapest ones he could find on Amazon), a hand torch (just in case), plenty of spare batteries, and finally the maps and plans he had acquired from the old man in the pub. Oh, and the big brass key.

***

If there was one word that could be used to sum up the brilliant, bullish, passionate, loyal, headstrong, intelligent, generous and infinitely-loving being known to her friends as Roz, it was 'sharp'. Absolutely nothing got by her. She could read her fellow human beings as easily as others read takeaway menus. Friends, associates and strangers were as open to her as flowers, and of this one thing she was certain: Syeeda was keeping something back.

Since they had both breezed into Jason's cafe that morning, Rosalind had sensed that her young friend had been on the verge of imparting something. The fact that she had not done so as yet meant that it was probably something important. But in addition to all her other attributes, Rosalind was also patient, and was content to wait until Syeeda felt that the time was right.

"So do you know Rich's other half well?" Ffion asked Syeeda.

"Yeah, pretty well," Syeeda replied. "I see her in yoga every week. She's really nice but there's no way I'd ever have put the two of them together."

"My eldest calls it Yoda," chuckled Ffion. "It's so cute."

"That is pretty cute."

"So does yoga actually work?" asked Rosalind. "I've been thinking of giving it a go."

Syeeda's face became serious. "Oh yeah. Absolutely." She nodded. "You should see my arms now. They're pretty ripped."

"I'm hoping it might offset all the wine I drink."

"Do you reckon it could sort *me* out?" asked Ffion, patting her soft belly.

"Definitely," said Syeeda. "If you go regularly and cut back on the full Englishes a bit, you'd be amazed how fast you tone up."

"Will it help me grow any taller?"

"No. Can't help you with that one, I'm afraid."

"Pity. I was hoping it would make me look more glamorous when I'm standing next to you."

Syeeda screwed her face up. "What are you on about, Fee? You're gorgeous!"

"Am I balls!" Ffion exclaimed. "Look how short and fat I am."

"So?" Rosalind butted in. "I can tell you for a fact that pretty much all the heterosexual males in our circle have got the hots for you."

Jason's ears pricked up.

"What? Really?" Ffion asked with genuine surprise.

18

"Yep. Christ, even I look at you sometimes and think, 'I would'."

Ffion nearly choked on her tea. She turned to Syeeda who cocked an eyebrow and nodded. She felt her cheeks turning beetroot.There was a moment or two of silence, and then Syeeda decided to break it. "If you were a crisp,what kind of crisp would you be?"

"Where on earth has *that* come from?" asked a baffled Rosalind.

"I don't know. We were talking about it in work the other day. If you were a crisp, what kind of crisp would you be? I said I'd be a Twiglet cos I'm so skinny."

"I can honestly say I've never really thought about it," said Rosalind.

"How about you, Fee?"

"Hmmm. A Space Raider."

"Really? Why?"

"Well, you know how much I love science fiction films. Anything with aliens in it I love, so I'd have to go for a Space Raider."

"Makes sense. Roz, have you decided yet?"

"No. Pass."

"You can't pass," said Syeeda. "You're not usually afraid of commitment."

"Is there any such thing as a clever crisp? If there is, that's what you'd be," said Ffion.

"Thanks, Fee,"

"What's the poshest kind of crisp you can get?" said Syeeda, stirring the pot. "That's the kind of crisp she'd be."

"Oi!" said Rosalind. "Less of the posh!"

"Morning, ladies," said a familiar voice. "Are we all ready?"

"You can wait till I've finished my sodding breakfast first, Rich," said Ffion.

Rich ordered a latte and took a seat. The conversation flowed easily and merrily as the four friends contemplated their upcoming adventure together. By late afternoon, however, only one of them would still be alive.

Chapter Two

Morning frost still sparkled on what remained of the old platforms and buildings. A wide trench carrying train tracks cut through the debris-strewn site, ending abruptly at the two bricked-up tunnels in the hillside.

As the party approached, a fox darted stealthily away. From here, the usual cacophony of London traffic was relegated to a low, distant hum. The only sounds that truly registered came from the crows that, unused to human interlopers, cawed and flapped in agitation.

Rosalind ran her hand along one of the platforms, her fingertips skating across the frozen moss. She spent her working life surrounded by history; books and ledgers and records and maps and documents, but this was the kind of history that she truly loved, the kind that she could touch, smell, explore, sense. In such places, she felt a distant, ghostly connection to all the souls who had passed by before her.

"I've heard of this place but never been here," she said, her breath vaporising in front of her nose.

"Yep. This is the old Highgate Train Station. The one I told you about," said Rich. "According to the plans, we should be able to access the deep level from here."

"What's a deep level?" asked Ffion. Nobody answered her.

Rich delved into his rucksack and carefully, reverentially, pulled out a video camera.

"That looks expensive," Syeeda remarked.

"Very," Rich flatly confirmed. Actually, he had got a pretty good deal on it, but he wanted to revel in her momentary awe.

Ffion's face appeared in a long-gone window in one of the

derelict buildings. "Hey, Syd," she called. "Have you ever shagged in a train station waiting room?"

"What? No!" exclaimed a shocked Syeeda.

"No. Nor me," Ffion sheepishly responded.

Syeeda's phone had been in her hand since they had arrived. When she was sure that Rosalind wasn't looking, she held it up in front of her, raised aloft two fingers to form a V, pouted, and snapped a quick selfie.

"Right then," said Rich, addressing Rosalind. "Do you know what you're going to say?"

"No," Rosalind shrugged. "Haven't a clue."

"Oh, for goodness sake. I asked you to prepare something for the intro."

"Then you shouldn't have been so vague about what you wanted. You gave me nothing to go on."

"But you're into history, AND you work in the archives.You should know this stuff anyway."

"Just because I work in the archives doesn't mean I know every little scrap of information about every historical thing ever. I do have to research things, you know."

"Yes, and I asked you to research this."

"No you didn't. You just said to come up with something about the old Highgate Station for the intro. That's hardly what I would call defining project parameters."

"Hang on a mo," said Syeeda, stepping forward, mobile in hand. Rich and Rosalind shuffled their feet while she swiped away at the screen. "How about this?" she said eventually. "Highgate is a London underground station and former train station in Archway Road, in the London borough of Haringey."

"Where's that from?" Rich asked.

"Wikipedia."

"Well we can't just pinch our intro verbatim from Wikipedia. We've got to make it look like we've put some effort into it."

"What else does it say?" Rosalind asked.

"The station was originally opened in 1867 as part of the great northern..."

"Right, that'll do," said Rosalind. "Give that here and I'll quickly absorb a few facts."

Syeeda smirked. "I thought you didn't like smartphones."

"Hey, Roz," said Ffion. "Did you know that the London underground is one of the most haunted places in the world?"

Rosalind was sceptical. "Oh, really? Where did you get that from?"

"Saw it on the telly."

"Hm."

"I'll film it from here, I think," said Rich, forming a frame with his fingers and thumbs and squinting through them. "Looking down the old line with the tunnels in the background. Mmm."

"Ha! Look at Steven Spielberg by 'ere." Ffion laughed. Rich ignored her.

"So how do we get in?" Syeeda asked, looking around.

"Through one of those," Rich replied, pointing at the tunnels. They were bricked up only to a certain point, so that the top of each arc remained open.

"You're having a laugh," gasped Ffion. "I'll never get my arse through there!"

"So how do we get in?" Syeeda asked again, this time with a hint of sarcasm.

Rich was growing impatient. "By helping each other."

"Well, I suppose we could pile a few of those pallets up," said Rosalind, ever practical, "then we don't have so far to climb."

"We can give each other a leg up," Syeeda chipped in.

"What I'm more worried about," said Ffion, "is how the fuck we're going to get back out."

Completely oblivious to everything that had just been said, Rich continued to fiddle with his video camera.

"Oi! Dickhead!" barked Ffion witha cheeky grin. "Any chance we can get a move on? I'm bastard freezing, mun!"

"Alright, alright," mumbled Rich without looking up. "Let's go for a take."

"Ooh, let's go for a take," Ffion cheerfully mocked.

"Right then," said Rich, snapping into director-mode.

"Let's have the three of you standing here on the tracks with the tunnels behind. Rosalind, you can introduce everyone, give us a bit of spiel about the history of the place and then gesture to the tunnels and say something like, '...and somewhere down there lies the fabled deep level, a forgotten underground train network built during the Victorian era'."

"Mm hm," affirmed Rosalind.

"And then you go, 'Okay, let's go'. And then you all walk off towards the tunnels. Got it?"

Syeeda and Ffion nodded blankly while Rosalind stared intensely ahead.

Must be her concentrating face, thought Rich.

The three stars lined up shoulder-to-shoulder with the tunnels behind.

"Okay then," said Rich. "Are you sure you're all ready?"

"Oh, just get on with it," Ffion grumbled.

Rich lifted the video camera up to his face and squinted at the small viewfinder. His thumb fumbled around in search of the record button. "Aaaaaand ACTION!"

"Sorry, what do I say, again?" asked Rosalind.

"Oh, for fuck's sake!" snapped Rich, dropping the camera down from his face.

"It was a joke! It was a joke," pleaded Rosalind. The three of them all burst into laughter.

Rich sighed and took it on the chin. "Okay, okay," he conceded. "Very good. When you've quite finished."

"Okay, I'm ready now," said Rosalind, pulling herself together. "Honest."

Rich lifted the camera back up.

"Ooh! Before we start," said Syeeda, "how about a group shot." She rushed forward, handed her phone to Rich, and then trotted back to the line-up.

Rich rolled his eyes and sighed. "Okay. Ready?"

Rosalind continued to glare straight ahead, Ffion smiled and Syeeda put her hands on her hips, struck a pose and pouted.

"Got it," said Rich.

"Thanks, Rich," said Syeeda, taking her phone back.

"Right then. Can we get on? Take two. ACTION!"

Rosalind snapped into presenter-mode. "Hi. I'm Rosalind, this is Syeeda and this is Ffion."

Syeeda tried to look cool while Ffion gave a little wave to the camera.

Perfect, thought Rich.

"The London underground is the oldest underground train network in the world. It's also one of the most haunted places in the world."

Ffion grinned smugly.

"It is a place of history and great mysteries, and that is what has brought us here today. We're standing in what's left of Highgate Train Station, opened in 1867 as part of the Great Northern Railway's Northern Heights plan."

Man, she's good!

"Somewhere far below us," Rosalind continued, "lies a fabled underground train network, built in secret during the Victorian era, utilised during the Second World War as a bomb shelter, and then sealed up and forgotten...until now."

Oh, yeah! This is dynamite!

"Why this network was built in the first place, nobody knows, but no human being has set foot in there for over seventy years. We have no idea what awaits us down there in the depths, but today...we aim to find out, and we want you to come with us."

Keep it up, baby! Keep it up!

"The only way in is through those tunnels." Rosalind gestured toward the arches in the background. "They have long since been bricked up, but it's going to take more than a few bricks to put us off. Isn't that right, ladies?"

Taken by surprise and wide-eyed, Syeeda and Ffion muttered some affirmatives.

"Okay. Let's go exploring." And, led by Rosalind, the three of them turned their backs to the camera and walked off towards their goal.

"Aaaand CUT!" shouted Rich. "That was AMAZING! Roz, you were fantastic! What a natural!"

"Well, one doesn't like to brag."

"No, seriously, that was ace! Just what I wanted. Brilliant."

"Right," said Ffion, interrupting. "Are we getting on with this then, is it or what?"

"Yes. Hm." Rich started looking around. "Why don't we gather up a few of those pallets and pile them up by the entrance? That should make it easier to get in."

"Brilliant idea," said Rosalind. "Why didn't I think of that?"

"But remember, guys," said Rich, "it's safety first, okay? We absolutely cannot afford for this camera to get damaged."

His three friends rolled their eyes. Within minutes, several pallets had been gathered and stacked up against one of the tunnel entrances.

"This is starting to look a lot more doable," said Rich.

"Speak for yourself," said Ffion.

"With any luck," Rich continued, "there should be something in there we can stand on to get back out."

"That's what I like about you," said Rosalind. "You always plan everything so meticulously."

"Right. So Syd, you're the tallest so you go over first."

Syeeda didn't like the sound of this.

"Then, Roz, you go up. And while you're still up there, I'll pass my backpack up to you and you carefully pass it down to Syd on the other side."

"You and that sodding bag," said Ffion.

"Then Syd can help you down the other side," said Rich, ignoring her.

"Who's going to help *me* down?" asked Syeeda.

"You'll just have to improvise. Then I'll give you a leg up, Fee, and then I'll come over last."

"You're not coming over me," Ffion quipped.

"Oh my days," squealed Syd. "I think I'm going to be sick!"

Ffion let loose a dirty laugh.

"Come on then," said Rosalind. "Let's hustle."

Syeeda, being so tall, did not need much of a leg up. She mounted the brick wall with ease, and slowly started to lower herself down the other side.

"Good job I'm fit," she said.

"Careful, Syd!" Ffion yelled.

Syeeda's face disappeared behind the brick wall.

"Yes, be careful," Rosalind echoed.

From inside, there came a short scream followed by a crash.

"Syeeda," cried Rosalind and Ffion.

Rich's eyes widened with concern. He saw his great plan ending before it had even begun.

"I'm alright," came a little voice from inside the tunnel. "Just a tiny mishap."

Rosalind and Ffion looked to each other and breathed great big sighs of relief.

"Okay, Roz," said Rich. "You're up."

Rich cupped his hands, Rosalind placed her left foot into them, and with a great push she was levitated up to the top of the wall.

"Ooh, fucking 'ell," she wheezed.

"You okay, Roz?" asked Ffion.

"I'm fine," she said. "Syd, what night's your yoga class on again?"

"Tuesdays," came the faint response from the darkness.

There wasn't a lot of room between the roof of the tunnel and the top of the wall so Rosalind couldn't straighten herself up.

"Here comes the bag," said Rich. "Be very, very careful. There's a lot of very expensive equipment in here."

"Yeah, like his sandwiches," said Ffion.

Rosalind took the backpack. "Oi! Syeeda," she said. "CATCH!"

"NO!" yelled Rich with genuine terror.

Rosalind exploded with laughter. "Oh, for goodness sake, Rich! As if I would."

Rich's entire body seemed to deflate as he sighed. "Please don't do that to me again," he pleaded with his hand on his heart.

"Okay, Syd," said Rosalind. "Here comes the precious bag."

"Got it."

"And here comes not-so-precious me." Slowly, awkwardly, Rosalind started to lower herself down.

Rich winced as the sound of another crash echoed from the other side of the wall.

"Everyone okay?"

"Fine."

"Good."

"Smells in here."

"Fee. Your turn."

"Oh, god," said Ffion. "Am I allowed to change my mind?"

"NO!" echoed two voices from inside the tunnel.

"Right," said Ffion. "Let's get on with it then."

Rich cupped his hands.

"Christ! I can't get my leg up that high. Lower, mun."

Rich lowered his cupped hands and Ffion placed a wobbly foot into them.

"Three – two – one," said Rich, and heaved her up.

Ffion, stretching out her arms, managed to get her fingertips onto the top of the wall. "You'll have to do better than that, Rich," she croaked.

There was nothing else for it. Rich put his hands onto her bum and pushed.

"Whooooaaah!" Ffion blurted out as she found herself catapulted upwards.

Rich looked on in horror as Ffion tumbled straight over the top of the wall and down the other side. There followed several screams and another crash.

"Everyone okay?"

"RICH! YOU TWAT!" Ffion yelled from the darkness.

Richard ignored her. "Right then!" he shouted. "Here I come!"

Taking a deep breath, he jumped as high as he could manage, caught hold of the top of the wall and hauled himself up.

"Ready?" he asked.

"Ready," came the response. And he lowered himself down into the unknown.

Chapter Three

"Who's got the bag?" asked Rich.

There was no answer, save for the echo of dirty water drip drip dripping.

The vast, cavernous space was illuminated by two shards of light cutting in through all that remained of the tunnel entrances. Rich squinted as his eyes adjusted to the darkness. Suddenly there was movement, and he saw a shadowy figure reaching out towards him. He felt a chill.

"Take it then," the voice of Ffion suddenly snapped, causing numerous pigeons to coo and flap.

Still in a state of mild bewilderment, he took the backpack from his friend. "Ta," he said.

"Don't suppose you've got any torches in there, have you?"

"Funny you should mention it." Rich undid the zip and blindly rummaged around inside. "Here," he said, holding something vaguely towards Ffion.

"What do I do with this?" she asked, taking it.

"Strap it around your head and switch it on."

"I'll help you," said Rosalind. "Me and Phil use these when we go camping."

"Here's yours," said Rich to Syeeda.

"Thanks."

Suddenly there was illumination.

"Cool," said Ffion as she spun her head around, casting a pool of light over the wet, mossy surfaces.

"Watch out for ghosties," Rosalind whispered in her ear.

"Aw, don't!" Ffion cried. "I hate ghosties!"

"Where'd you get these from?" asked Syeeda, as she fumbled around looking for the switch.

"Amazon," replied Rich. "Roz."

"Cheers."

Syeeda's light came on. "Yay! This is awesome," she cheered. "Can I keep mine?"

"If you want."

"Yeah. If you make it out alive," laughed Rosalind.

"Hey, girls," said Ffion. "Watch this." She took the lamp from her head and stuck it into her mouth, causing her cheeks to glow bright orange.

Rosalind and Syeeda erupted into laughter.

"I'll have a go," said Syeeda. "Take a photo of me." She handed her phone to Ffion and stuck her lamp in her mouth.

"What do I press?" asked Ffion. "Hang on. I've got it." The phone flashed, temporarily blinding everyone.

"Thanks," said Syeeda, taking it back and looking at the picture. "Fabio."

"What the hell is that?" gasped Ffion.

Everyone looked at her, and then from her to Rich.

"What? This?" he said as casually as possible. "Night vision gear, as used by the SAS."

"Will they fit over your glasses?" Ffion asked.

"Yeah. Took them for a test run last night. Walked around the block after it'd got dark."

"You actually walked around in public wearing those?" Syeeda chuckled. "I'd have paid to see that."

"So how come you've got night vision gear as used by the SAS and we've got head torches from Amazon?" asked Rosalind.

"Because I'm the one doing the filming. And speaking of which, gather round everyone, it's time to do our next segment. Roz, you'll need this." And from his bag, Rich pulled out and unfolded a very large sheet of yellowing paper.

"Yay," said Syeeda. "Still got signal." Clearly, she wasn't paying any attention to what was going on, proving the point that Rosalind had made in the cafe earlier that morning.

"What's that?" Rosalind asked.

"It's a map," replied Rich. "The one that's going to guide

29

us to the deep level."

"I see. And this came from where exactly?"

"Long story. And ACTION!"

"Hang on a minute," snapped Rosalind. "What am I supposed to say now?"

Rich sighed. "Just say that that's the map that's going to guide you down to the deep level, and that..."

"Okay, okay. I've got it. Come on then."

"Right. Action."

Rosalind held the map up to camera. "This is the map that's going to guide the three of us deep underground where, hopefully, we'll find a secret network of underground train tunnels, originally built by the Victorians. They've been lying undisturbed since the days of the Second World War, and we..."

"Fuckin' 'ell! There's a rat!" screamed Ffion.

"Oh my days!" Syeeda gasped. "Where?"

"Over there! Behind Rich!"

"I can't see it!"

"Shall we cut there?" asked Rosalind.

"No, this is perfect," said Rich.

"Shall I carry on then?"

"Yes. Go on." Through Rich's viewfinder his three friends were monochrome and ghostly.

"The tunnels have been lying undisturbed since the Second World War, and we are here to uncover the secrets of this mysterious...deep level."

And with that, Rosalind, Syeeda and Ffion turned and started to walk away. Rich filmed until they had disappeared into the dark grey haze.

"That's it. Cut!"

"Sorry, Rich," said Ffion. "I freaked out there when I saw that rat."

"That's okay," said Rich. "I want to catch all that stuff. It'll make the doc more interesting."

"Are you going to film us having a wee and all?"

Rich was taken aback. "No," he stated flatly.

"That's okay then, cos I need one right now. Where can I

go?"

"Just find a dark corner somewhere," said Rosalind. "It's not like we'll be able to see you."

"Well, Rich can with his night vision thingies."

"Here, I'm switching it off," said Rich.

In the gloom, Ffion heard the faint sound of something electrical powering down.

"Right then," said Ffion. "I'll be back in a mo. Nobody go shining torches at me."

"I can honestly say that I have absolutely no desire to see you urinating," mumbled Syeeda from somewhere in the darkness.

"Right. Promise me that no one's gonna shine their torches at me when I'm weeing."

"Oh, just get on with it!" cried everyone.

Noisily, clumsily and casting a pool of light that ricocheted around the great, black, cathedral-like cavern, Ffion bumbled away to find somewhere private.

"Don't go off anywhere until I come back!" she yelled.

"We won't," said everyone wearily.

"Shall we hide?" whispered Syeeda.

"Oh no. Better not," replied Rosalind. "She'll freak out."

"Mm."

"I need to suss out which tunnel we're taking," said Rich from somewhere or another. "And then I can get some shots of you leading with the map, Roz."

"I thought you'd sussed all that out beforehand."

"I did. But everything looks so much different in the dark."

"You're not wrong there."

"I can't believe how cold it is," said Syeeda. "I'm so glad I brought my fleece."

"Cold, damp, dank and dark," said Rosalind. "What a perfect way to spend a Saturday morning."

A shriek echoed through the darkness.

"Ffion!" called Rosalind. "Are you okay?"

"I'm okay," came a little voice from the gloom. "I just fell on my arse, that's all."

Rich eventually managed to figure out which tunnel to take. "Okay, follow me, girls," he said.

Rosalind winced at being addressed as 'a girl', but she followed as Rich led her and her friends into a long straight passageway that seemed to go on forever.

"Okay," said Rich, readying his camera. "Roz, if you want to lift the map up a bit there. That's it. So, when I say 'action', I want you to pretend that you're studying the map and then say that this is the way you need to go and then you lead Syd and Fee down that way, right?"

"Right."

"Aaaand, ACTION!"

There was a moment's silence and then,"BOO!"

Syeeda and Ffion screamed and jumped.

"Hah. Gotcha," chuckled Rosalind.

"ROZ, MUN!" cried Ffion. "I nearly shit myself then!"

Syeeda just shook her head. "So cruel. So cruel."

This was exactly the kind of thing Rich wanted, the personalities of his three friends shining through as they uncovered a great Victorian mystery. *This is what's going to get people logging on*, said the voice inside his head. He then realised that he hadn't given his wife or daughter a moment's thought since he had left his flat.

The scene was filmed and the three friends, with circles of light flying around everywhere, began edging their way along the passage. Rich tailed behind, camera on standby.

"When's this tunnel going to end?" said Syeeda, without expecting a serious answer.

"Never," said Rosalind. "We've all actually died, and this is how we're going to spend eternity."

"Fuckin' 'ell, Roz," said Ffion. "You're on one today."

"Ooh. What's this?" Rosalind stopped suddenly causing Syeeda and Ffion to bump into the back of her. "Oi, Rich. There's another tunnel here."

"Oh, right. Brilliant. Didn't think we'd get here this soon. Okay. Let's back up and I'll film you discovering the tunnel and then going off down it."

"What do you mean 'down'?" said Syeeda.

"There should be steps here going down to the next level, and below that should be the deep level. So I just want to get some footage of you heading in through the tunnel entrance and..."

"These steps don't look very safe," said Ffion, aiming her head torch into the blackness.

Rich ignored her. "Okay, Roz, everyone, are you ready?"

"No, seriously. They're tiny and they look slippery."

"Oh, can we just get on with it, please?" Rich pleaded with impatience, rolling his eyes in the dark.

"Hey, Rich," said Ffion. "What's the most unusual object you've ever had shoved up your arse?"

Rich was quite taken aback. "I've never had anything shoved up my arse. Why?"

"Because that camera's about to be."

Rich realised that in losing patience with Ffion he'd crossed a line. "Okay. Okay. I'm sorry. I hear what you're saying about the steps. We just need to take our time and be careful, that's all. It'll be fine. Right, shall we go for a take?"

Rosalind, Syeeda and Ffion all put their serious faces on and turned to camera.

"So, Roz, you just say something like, 'We've discovered another passageway, one that leads down into the depths. If the map is right, this should lead us down to the next level. 'Got that?"

"Yeah. Piece of piss."

"Okay. ACTION!"

"Why does he have to shout that all the time?" said Ffion. "We're standing right here."

Rosalind began. "We've discovered a new tunnel here," she said."One that we were not expecting to find so soon. Looking in, I can see that it heads downwards very steeply. If the map is correct, this should lead us down to the next level. And there, somewhere, should be the entrance to the mysterious deep level."

Rosalind then turned and led her friends into the gloom.

"Amazing!" yelled Rich. "Roz, I can't believe how good you are at this! You should be a TV presenter."

"You should, actually," Syeeda agreed.

"Well..." Rosalind smiled, slightly embarrassed.

"Is it time for a tea break yet?" asked Ffion.

"No," said Rich. "Let's press on."

He filmed his three friends slowly negotiating the small, wet, slippery steps down into the unknown. As they descended, the air grew progressively colder.

"Jesus, mun," exclaimed Ffion. "It's knobbling down here. Christ!"

"I've got my fleece AND my jacket on," said Syeeda, the cold air stinging her exposed face, "and I'm STILL shivering."

Keep it up, girls, thought Rich.

"I can see my breath freezing in the torch light," said Ffion. "Look." And to prove it, she exhaled deeply, sending a ghostly wisp of steam into the air.

Syeeda followed suit, breathing out a long sigh. "Oh yeah," she said.

"Come on," said Rosalind. "Let's keep moving."

"Aren't you cold, Roz?" asked Syeeda.

"Bloody frozen, so the sooner we find this bloody underground the sooner we can get out of here and go get some nice hot Americanos into us."

There were murmurs of agreement.

"Hang on a mo," said Rosalind. "I think I can see the end."

The gang emerged into the remains of a tube station platform.

"Beautiful," breathed Rosalind as she slowly explored this new space, this time capsule, with the pool of light from her head torch.

The station was as black and as still as a graveyard in the dead of night. There was no sound of dripping water, no echoes of scurrying rats, no pigeons; just a dank silence and a musty odour that permeated the air.

Standing here, in this still cavern, utterly devoid of light and warmth, far below the tides of people sweeping back and forth in the London streets far above, it occurred to Rosalind that this was quite possibly the first time that she had ever experienced pure silence.

Prior to this moment, what she had previously considered silence had actually been merely quiet. It had always been accompanied by a certain level of underlying sound, or, to borrow a phrase from her vinyl-collecting husband, surface noise.

No danger of any surface noise down here, she thought.

No, this was the complete absence of sound. No traffic, no voices, no movement, no birds, no rustling of leaves, no children, no dogs, no cats, no music, no wind, no rain, no rivers, no trees. This newly discovered silence was so precious it bordered on sacred, and none of the four wanted to be the first to trespass upon it. But breaths could not be held forever, and so...

"This is scary," whispered Ffion.

"Yeah," Syeeda quietly agreed.

Rosalind's circle of light rested on a metal bench on the platform. "Look at all this dust," she whispered. "Have you ever seen so much?"

"Roz," whispered Rich as he lifted the video camera to his eye. Or at least, to the nightvision gear that covered his eye.

"Oh yeah," said Roz as quietly as she could. She cleared her throat no louder than a mouse. "We've found our way down to an abandoned tube station. It looks like this place hasn't been disturbed in decades. Everything's covered by a layer of dust inches thick. Living in London, we never get to experience silence quite like this. It's actually ringing in my ears, which doesn't make sense, I know, but that's how it feels."

"Say something about how this isn't even as deep as you're going to go."

"Okay. Here goes. Ready? And believe it or not, we still haven't reached our destination. This old station is known about, it's charted, it has a history. But what we're looking for lies much deeper than this, and who knows what we're going to find down there?"

Rich lowered the camera. "Perfect," he breathed.

Rosalind noticed that her hands were shaking.

"Can we go now?" asked Ffion with a small gulp.

"Down to the deep level?" asked Rosalind.

"No. Home."

"No way," said Rich, still not daring to raise his voice above a croak. "Not now we're so close."

Despite the deafening stillness and the smell of decay, Rosalind longed for more. Like Rich, she shared the desire to step into the unknown, to uncover history.

"We're nearly there now," she soothed. "Only one more level down."

"I don't like this," said Syeeda. "I'm scared."

Rosalind placed a hand on Syeeda's arm. "Of what," she asked.

"I don't know. I'm just scared."

"Of ghosts?" asked Rich.

"Yes."

"Well, I wouldn't be if I were you. It's the living you've got to watch out for," he said.

"Yeah. Thanks, Rich," said Syeeda somewhat sarcastically.

"Aren't you scared then, Rich?" Ffion asked.

"No. I don't believe in ghosts, so as far as I'm concerned there's nothing down here *to* be afraid of. Apart from getting lost."

"Don't you believe in anything supernatural?" Syeeda asked.

"No, nothing. I think people jump to supernatural explanations far too quickly. It's just superstition."

"And how certain are you of that?" asked Rosalind with narrowed eyes.

"A hundred percent," replied Rich.

At that moment, Syeeda and Ffion, without knowing it, shared the same thought: *What's she up to?*

"Care to put that to the test?" Rosalind enquired.

Rich gulped. "What do you mean?"

"Are you up for us coming round to your house one night and doing a Ouija board?"

Rich was silent for a moment, and then eventually replied: "No. Marie would never let me."

"We'll do it when she's out."

"Yeah, she goes to yoga every week, doesn't she?" said Syeeda. "We can do it then."

The self-certainty that Rich usually carried in his voice evaporated, just like his breath in the cold air. "No. Best not."

"Why?" asked Rosalind slyly. "You're not afraid, are you?"

"Not at all. It's just that I don't think it's a good idea to do one round my house."

Rosalind had him on the run now. "What difference does it make? Nothing's going to happen. It's all just superstition after all, isn't it?"

"Well..."

"Well what?"

The noise was sharp and violent. In the moment of panic that followed, the three women grabbed at each other for safety as Rich stood motionless, staring dumbly at the murky monochrome image on his viewfinder. What had just happened?

Chapter Four

"Oh god oh god oh god oh god..." Ffion was gripping someone's arm tightly to her, but she didn't know whose.

"THERE!" Rich shouted.

Beams of light criss-crossed the cavern like wartime searchlights. Rich was focusing in on a rock. It was about the size of a man's fist. "I saw it move," he gasped. "Someone threw it."

Pulling herself away from her friends, Rosalind followed his line of vision and found it. "That?" she asked.

"Yes. I saw it rolling across the ground and stop there."

"Roz, I think we should go now," whispered Syeeda, wide-eyed and terrified. "I really, really think we should go."

"It's okay, Syd," said Rosalind, as calmly as she could as two beams of light dazzled her. "Either this just fell from the ceiling or there's someone else down here and they just want us to go away."

Ffion and Syeeda's voices rose as their last reserves of control gave way to naked fear. "There's someone down here I can feel it I know there is we have to go what if they can see us but we can't see them and they might be dangerous and they might be a psychopath and what if there's more and what if people come down here all the time and nobody knows because nobody ever gets back out and..."

Rich was filming everything.

Rosalind raised her voice to the level of her panic-stricken friends. "Woah woah woah! Don't get carried away! Come on, please!"

Ffion and Syeeda were still gripping each other tightly.

Rosalind continued. "If it *was* someone who threw that stone, they're obviously just nervous about us being here and would rather we left. I'm going to try calling to them."

"No, don't, Roz," Ffion frantically whispered. "Don't, don't, don't!"

Rosalind carried on regardless. "HELLOOOOOO! IS THERE ANYONE THERE?"

The noise bounced and echoed around the great cavern and down the tunnel and back again for what felt like minutes.

"HELLOOOOO!" she bellowed again. "WE'RE NOT HERE TO HURT YOU AND WE DON'T WANT TO CAUSE YOU ANY TROUBLE! WE'RE JUST HERE EXPLORING! IF THERE'S ANYONE THERE WHY NOT JUST COME AND SAY HELLO TO US? THERE'S NOTHING TO BE AFRAID OF!"

Eventually the echoes died away to leave behind a frozen silence. And then somebody somewhere coughed.

"Oh god oh god oh god oh god oh god."Syeeda and Ffion tightened their grips on each other. "Please can we go?" one of them whispered. "Please!"

Rich, still extremely nervous yet determined not to be the first one to abandon the mission, continued to film.

Rosalind felt as though her body temperature had dropped by about ten degrees. She was scared, but the cough that had found its way to them through the tunnel had gone some way to reassuring her, unlike her friends. It meant that yes, there was someone down here with them, but it was just a person, not a ghoul or a monster or a demon, just a lost soul perhaps, or a lonely outcast who wanted nothing more than to be left in peace.

"Roz. What are we going to do?" whispered Ffion.

"We have to go," added Syeeda. "We can't stay down here now."

"Roz? Roz?"

"Sh. I'm thinking."

"Roz," said Rich, butting in. "I think you need to say to the camera about what just happened here."

"Oh, bugger off, Richard," she snapped. And then, "Right. Here's what's going to happen..."

Rich put the camera up to his eye and pressed record.

"Somewhere down that tunnel is a modern-day hermit who for whatever reason is hiding from the world and clearly doesn't want to be found. Well, that's good, because it means that if we all just carry on with what we're doing – exploring – and follow the map to where we want to go and not go looking for any trouble, then they'll probably just stay out of our way..."

She was gabbling, which suggested to the others that she was a trifle more nervous than she was letting on.

"...so I think we need to be brave and stick together and carry on quietly and respectfully and keep bearing in mind that it's just a person down there..."

"But they lobbed a brick at us," Ffion retorted.

"Actually, it was a stone," said Syeeda.

"Oh, thanks a bunch," Ffion snarked. "I thought you were supposed to be on my side!"

A heated argument between Syeeda and Ffion thus ensued.

Rosalind turned to the camera. "So much for quietly and respectfully," she said with an arch of the eyebrow.

"Girls girls girls," Rich interjected. "This isn't helping. Roz is right. It's just a person down there and there's four of us, so there's nothing to be afraid of."

"How do you know there's just one person down there?" Syeeda demanded. "There could be hundreds of them."

"Because I only heard one cough."

"People don't all cough at the same time, you donk!" Ffion retorted.

Rosalind sighed. "Let me put it this way," she said, "I'm not going to let a stone and a cough put me off doing what I want to do, so I'm going to carry on. Now, who's with me? Rich?"

"Well, actually," said Rich, nodding towards the coughing tunnel, "according to the map, that's the way we've got to go anyway."

Syeeda and Ffion looked to Rosalind. She steeled herself and said: "Shall we?" and led the way. She lowered herself down from the platform onto the tracks and proceeded to walk off in the direction of the tunnel mouth.

Syeeda and Ffion gave each other a look and then followed.

***

"How much further, Rich?" Syeeda asked. "It feels like we've been walking forever."

"Actually, it's been about four minutes," Rosalind pointed out.

"It's hard to tell just by looking at the map," said Rich. "There wasn't a distance scale ratio thingy on it."

"Oh."

"It's a pretty long tunnel," he added."But we're not going all the way through. It veers off to the left to a service point, and that's where the entrance to the deep level is. I think."

"Well, that doesn't sound too bad," chirped Ffion. "Looks like I'll be home in time to go to Harvester after all."

"I still think you should let me come," said Syeeda.

"Bugger off," said Ffion with a slight chuckle.

There was a moment or two of silence, and then, "Got another question for you." It was Syeeda. "If you could uninvent something, what would it be?"

"Uninvent something?" said Ffion.

"Yeah."

"You're full of questions today, Syd," said Rosalind. "What's brought all this on?"

"Nothing. Just curious," she lied.

"Well. That's easy. The internet."

If anyone had been aiming a head torch in Syeeda's direction at the moment of Rosalind's statement, they would have seen the expression on her face migrate from mild interest to acute horror.

"The internet? But why?"

"Simply because I've seen the world become a worse place since it appeared."

"How's that then, Roz?" asked Ffion.

Rosalind took a deep breath. "Okay. Well. Once upon a

time you had all sorts of cranks and lunatics in the world – like flat-earthers, morons who think the world is run by a cabal of shape-shifting alien lizards and so on – all of whom were sitting in their bedrooms thinking that they were the only one. But now, the internet allows them to find each other, and the mere fact that there are other people out there who share their insane beliefs validates them. It emboldens them. And they think, I'm not the only one so I must be right.

"So now there's a movement of people who actually genuinely believe that the earth is flat, simply because there are other people out there who think the same. And it's not just cranks like flat-earthers and alien lizard conspiracy theorists. It's people with genuinely terrifying beliefs like white supremacists, holocaust deniers, paedophiles, men who think that rape doesn't qualify as a crime.

"The internet was supposed to liberate information and put it into the hands of everyone, but instead it's been used to proliferate lies and disinformation, and as a result, we actually have white supremacists in the White House. Just take a moment to let that sink in. Russia used social media to disseminate lies and wild conspiracy theories about Hillary Clinton in order to get their little puppet man into the White House. This could never have happened in the pre-internet era."

"Bloody hell," Ffion gasped. "I bet you're sorry you asked now. Eh, Syd?"

"So what about you, Fee? What would you uninvent?"

"Cling film."

"Cling film? What the..? But how can you..?"

"Ooh, I hates it, I do. It's just the way it sticks to everything and I can never just get it off the roll in a straight line. It always ends up all over the place. And I can never find the end of it. But when you've got to wrap things up to go in the fridge you've got no choice but to use it. And that's why I hate it. Because it's a massive pain in the arse but I can't do without it."

"Well, I'm convinced," said Rosalind.

"Yeah, me too," agreed Syeeda.

"So how about you then, Syd? You haven't told us what you'd uninvent."

"Easy. Spiders."

"You can't uninvent spiders," said Rosalind. "No one invented them. They evolved."

"I'd still uninvent them though."

"I hates spiders, I do," Ffion interjected. "I had one in the bath the other day that was so big it probably had its own National Insurance number."

The act of simply talking at a normal volume now was helping to dissipate the sense of fear and dread that had begun to weigh heavily upon the group. With every word confidently spoken, their spirits seemed to lift. By simply reintroducing something as simple as noise to this dark, cold, grave place, it gave them all the sense that some modicum of normality was present. If there were spirits here, they were in retreat. If there were other people here, they had better get used to the company. Breath no longer needed to be held.

Suddenly they all became aware of a ghostly blue glow. "Syeeda, is that you?" said Rosalind without turning around.

The glow disappeared. "Soz," Syeeda mumbled.

"Don't tell me you've still got signal down here."

"No," she conceded.

Rosalind was still thinking of Syeeda and pondering as to what her as yet undeclared news could be, and this reminded her that she had news of her own to impart. She cleared her throat and came right out with it: "Phil and I are putting the house on the market."

"What!" gasped Syeeda and Ffion. "You're moving away? To where?"

"Only a few doors up the road, so don't panic."

"What on earth for?" asked Ffion.

"Well, now that our boys have gone off to university, we want to make sure they never come back. So we're downsizing."

"That's terrible!" Syeeda blurted out.

"Yeah," agreed Ffion. "Fancy turning out your boys like that! I could never."

"We're hardly turning them out. As far as Phil and I are concerned, we've done our part. We've raised them well, they're intelligent, they're capable, so now they're on their own."

"Bloody hell! That's so harsh," exclaimed Ffion. "What about when they want to come and visit?"

"They can come and visit anytime," said Roz. "There's a guest room. We haven't completely turned our backs on them. But the days of living under someone else's roof are over."

"And what about Mr Darcy?" Syeeda implored. "He's going to be so confused!"

Mr Darcy was Rosalind and Phil's cat.

***

Rewind eight years. A soggy, bedraggled, ginger-haired moggy begins a long, lonely vigil on some randomly selected Acton doorstep. After five days of giving him the occasional bowl of food and water, the owners of said doorstep finally relent and open their house to him.

Rosalind: "We're going to name him Mr Darcy."

Phil: "Aha. I get it. You've decided that by calling him Mr Darcy he can represent for you some sort of unattainable male ideal."

Rosalind: "No. It's because cats are aloof, treat everyone around them with contempt and love hunting. Just like Mr Darcy from Pride and Prejudice."

Phil: "Fair enough."

***

"I never want my boys to leave home," said "Ffion. "They can stay with me for the rest of their lives if they want."

"Or the rest of yours, more to the point," cracked Syeeda.

"You say that now, Fee," said Rosalind, "but that's because they're still young. Still in the adorable stage."

"Not *that* bloody adorable," Ffion chuckled.

"How old are they now, Fee?" Syeeda asked.

"Iwan's gonna be five in March, Geraint's three in September,"

Rosalind chuckled. "There's something I've noticed about parents," she said. "Mums in particular – and I include myself in this too. They never tell you how old their children are now. They always say how old they're going to be on their next birthday."

"That is *so* true," said Syeeda.

"Do I do that?" Ffion asked, wearing the sheepish grin of someone who had just been well and truly found out.

"Yep," Rosalind chirped.

"I love their names," said Syeeda. "There's something about Welsh names. What's your mum's again?"

"Haulwyn."

"Beautiful."

"That *is* a nice name," agreed Rosalind. "The sort of name you could quite easily write a poem about."

"Hey, Syd," said Ffion cheerily. "Because me and Roz have both got boys, the responsibility's on you to have a girl."

"I think you're in for a long wait there," Syeeda stated firmly.

"Do I deduce from this that procreation is not on the immediate agenda then, Syd?" chuckled Rosalind.

"Absolutely not. Parenthood is my number one worst nightmare."

"What! Why?" Ffion asked.

"Because I like being able to do whatever I want, whenever I want. It's that simple."

"Very wise," said Rosalind. "But you would make a wonderful mother."

"I can just see you with a couple of beautiful daughters for my boys to get off with when they're older," Ffion added.

Rosalind and Syeeda both gasped. Actually, so did Rich. By now he had become a ghostly presence, ever present but silent and almost invisible. The three ladies had all but forgotten that he was there, which was exactly what he

45

wanted.

"Was it something I said?" Ffion asked.

For the record, Rosalind had been right about Syeeda. She did indeed have news, but it was good news, *very* good news, and she was relishing the warm, tingly feeling of carrying it around with her. In her head she had already rehearsed how she was going to share this news with her friends, but right at this moment, for all the scares and the cold and the smell of decay, she was simply enjoying being with them on an adventure. Their presence made her feel strong, like she was part of something bigger. She would tell them her news when they were once again standing in daylight. That would be the happy ending that this day deserved.

"Hey, Roz," said Syeeda, still in the mood for questions. "Have you decided what kind of crisp you are yet?"

"Oh, yeah," said Ffion. "I'd forgotten about that. Come on, Roz, you've got to pick a crisp."

"Oh, god. We're back to that again now, are we?"

"Yep," said a mischievous Syeeda. "I wasn't going to let something as important as this go. You have to make a decision. What kind of crisp are you?"

"Something as important as this, indeed," Rosalind mocked. "For goodness sake."

"Come on. Crisp," Ffion demanded.

And just as Rosalind was trying to formulate a plan to extricate herself from this topic of conversation, something in the darkness appeared.

"Ooh, look at this. The tunnel's veering off to the left here. Just like you said, Rich."

Camera on standby, thought Rich. "Yeah. This could be it. Right then. To the left."

Rich was not someone given over to smiling lightly. Rosalind, Syeeda and Ffion often joked that they had never actually seen him crack one. They would all tell him stupid jokes to try and induce him but to no avail. But right now, the prospect of what awaited him down here in the cold, deep, dark excited him enough to cause a wry, self-satisfied smile to break across his face. Unfortunately, however, because of that very same darkness, nobody saw it.

His goal was close enough now to cause a flutter of butterflies in his belly. It was somewhere in the nearby service point that the entrance to the deep level was hidden. He noticed that his hands had started shaking slightly, and then he bumped into the back of Ffion.

"So what's a service point then, Rich?" asked Ffion.

"It's somewhere where the trains went to get serviced," replied Rich from the rear. "There'll probably be an engineering workshop there or something."

"Sounds interesting," said Rosalind as she continued to lead the group along this new tunnel.

"Mmm," Ffion quietly agreed.

On any other day, the thought of exploring a greasy, oily old workshop where trains were once serviced would have induced yawns in Ffion, but this was different. It was a service point deep underground in a forbidden place which may or may not be inhabited by escapees from the world above. Despite the frights and the cold and the dark, she was, like her friend Syeeda, actually enjoying the experience. It occurred to her that the horrors she had encountered so far on this little expedition were pretty minor compared to the ones that she had to endure up there in the normal world every single day. Horrors such as the rent, the late working hours and the daily commute.

If she had to choose between a deathly cold, graveyard-black, abandoned tube station swirling with ghosts in the dead of night, or Leicester Square tube station strangled with the living at 6:30 on a Monday evening, she would enthusiastically plump for the former. The constant darkness, something she had previously feared, had heightened her senses to a degree previously unknown. Every atom in her body was on full-alert and she felt vital and alive in this strange netherworld.

From somewhere in the darkness there came a low rumbling sound.

"Fee," said Syeeda. "Was that your stomach?"

"Yeah," conceded Ffion. "I'm starting to get hungry."

"What? After that enormous breakfast you had?"

"That was hours ago."

"Well tell it to be quiet."

The tunnel opened out into a vast cavern and everyone suddenly stopped dead.

"What's going on?" said Rich.

"You might want to come and have a look at this,"breathed Rosalind.

Chapter Five

This was more than just a cavern, it was an underworld, a subterranean kingdom; huge, open and grand. The three circles of light from the head torches slowly, tentatively swept and dived around this exciting new space, exploring every corner and crevice.

"It's like a graveyard," Rich mumbled.

A tangle of tracks spread out in wild directions before the four friends. And on the tracks, silently resting, was a fleet of rusting Victorian engines. Treading carefully along one of the tracks, Rosalind made her way to the nearest one.

"Roz," said Rich. "Say something." He raised his camera and pressed record and a little red dot flashed into life. However, silence had once again claimed dominion and Rosalind could find no appropriate words.

"Roz," Rich prompted with a whisper. "We're rolling."

Unbidden, Syeeda and Ffion both walked over to stand shoulder to shoulder with their friend.

"Roz," whispered Rich once again.

Rosalind opened her mouth and pushed out some words, hoping that they would be the right ones. They were. "This is incredible," she began. "We've stumbled upon something that none of us expected to find here today, a graveyard of old Victorian steam trains. It looks like there's about a dozen here plus the carriages. I don't know how many of those there are, but it's a lot."

Rich panned his camera across the scene. In shades of ghostly grey, he saw decaying hulks of varying shapes and sizes. In comparison to above-ground steam trains they were small, but they still dwarfed their human visitors.

"It's impossible to say how long these engines and

carriages have lain here untouched," Rosalind continued. "But it's probably been since the Second World War when this place was used as a bomb shelter."

She placed a hand upon the hull of one of the engines. It was a very basic design, comprising a large boiler with a stumpy chimney protruding from the top, a small footplate where once a driver would have stood, and four large wheels.

"Once upon a time this place would have been alive with people and activity, and the noise would have been deafening. But today, it's as silent as a tomb."

"Perfect," breathed Rich. "Thank you, Roz."

Quietly, the group of four spread out amongst the rusting metal beasts to explore and touch. Rosalind noticed that the engines all had nameplates. Agatha, read one. Prunella, read another. Meanwhile, Rich was filming his slow journey. He panned up and down and left and right, capturing as much detail as he could of these forgotten hulks.

There was a scream. The scream was immediately followed by nervous laughter.

"Sorry," Ffion called out, her voice echoing off the arcing brickwork high above. "Me and Syd scared each other."

"I think we'd better stick together," whispered Syeeda, taking Ffion's hand. They followed a set of tracks as they twisted between two lines of great, rusting engines.

"This is sooo creepy," Ffion said in a whisper even the keen ears of a dog would have struggled to detect. However, she had said it with a relishing smile.

"I know," Syeeda replied. She slipped her phone from her pocket and started taking photos.

"Psst. Rich. Come and see this," said Rosalind. She didn't actually know where Rich was, but the cavernous space carried her voice through all the engines until it reached his ears.

"Roz?"

"Over here."

A moment later, the tell-tale red light on Rich's camera bobbed into view.

"Look at this," Rosalind said again.

Through his viewfinder, Rich saw Rosalind pointing at the nameplate on one of the engines.

"It's called Rosalind," she said. "Isn't that amazing?"

"Yes," said Rich. "That actually is amazing. We'll have to get that on film. Do you know what you're going to say?"

"I can't believe there's actually a train with my name on it."

"Roz, are you ready?"

"What? Oh yes. Go on then."

"Roz! Rich! You have to see this!" It was Syeeda. Her voiced echoed and bounced around the vast, dark cavern, making it impossible to pinpoint where she was.

"Where are you?" called Rosalind.

"Over here!"

"Not much help!"

Rich put his hand on Rosalind's shoulder and pointed towards two beams of light.

"Oh yes. Got you!" cried Rosalind. "Hang on a mo." Before leaving, she placed the palm of her right hand gently on the engine that shared her name and bade it a silent goodbye.

Syeeda and Ffion had found their way onto a platform at the far end of the space. Parked at the platform was a long, wooden train carriage, dusty and decrepit. They were both peering in through one of the windows.

"You're not going to believe this," said Ffion.

Rosalind clambered up onto the platform, followed by Rich. Rich was still filming.

"Look," said Syeeda.

It was hard to see in through the carriage window because of the reflection from her head torch, but through the layers of dust and cobwebs, Rosalind could just about make out..."Are those blankets? And clothes? I can see a coat and shoes and..."

"And candles, look," Ffion added. "And books."

"Rich, are you getting this?" Rosalind asked.

"I am," he breathed. This was all so much more than he had hoped for.

"Roz," he prompted.

Rosalind turned to the camera. "Here amongst the rusty old engines we've found what appears to be a makeshift dwelling. Inside we can see old clothes, blankets, even candles. Someone *is* living down here. Or perhaps several people. Was it one of them that threw the stone at us earlier?"

Damn, she's good!

"I'm going to try calling out to see if anyone answers."

"Roz, no." It was Ffion.

"It's alright, Fee," Roz reassured her. "There's nothing to be afraid of, I promise you."

"But..."

"Hello! Is there anyone here with us," Rosalind called out. "We don't mean you any harm! We just want to talk to you!"

"Sounds just like Most Haunted," sniggered Syeeda.

"It does, dunnit?" agreed Ffion. "Is there anybody there?" she called out in a mocking, ghostly voice.

"Ffion!" Rosalind snapped. "Behave."

Ffion and Syeeda both laughed like two wicked schoolgirls caught in the wrong kind of act. This was exactly what Rich wanted, the spontaneous interplay that only occurs between the truest of friends.

"I'm going to have a look inside," said Syeeda as she reached out for the carriage door. The laughter and the camaraderie had helped to dissipate her fear. However she was prevented from entering by Ffion, who had put a hand on Syeeda's arm.

"Don't, Syd," she said. "It's someone's home. You wouldn't like it if someone went nosing around in your home."

"I'm only going to have a quick look," said Syd. She shrugged Ffion's hand from her arm and turned the handle. The door was lighter than she expected and the wood rotten and crumbly.

Rosalind, Ffion and Rich competed to be the loudest and most desperate: "Oh god! Close it! Close it, Syd! Jesus Christ!"

The sickly-warm stench of human faeces and urine had

wafted swiftly and pungently over the party. Eyes were narrowed, faces were scrunched, tears were streamed. Syeeda slammed the door shut, causing chunks of wood to fall away.

"Jesus effing Christ, mun!" Ffion gasped. "I've never smelt anything like that in my life! And I've had two kids!"

"I'm really sorry," Syeeda pleaded. "I didn't think it was..."

"It smells like the devil's armpit in there!"

"It's alright, Syd," said Rosalind, cutting Ffion off. "Come on. Whoever's here obviously doesn't want to be found. Let's just leave him or her alone."

"Yeah," said Ffion. "Any chance we can go find this sodding deep level now then, Rich, is it or what?"

Rich, who had been filming the whole thing, lowered his camera. "Yeah. Let's get down to business," he said firmly as he took off his backpack. "Somewhere in here is the entrance we're looking for. Let's see what we can see."

He fished an A4 plastic folder from his bag, slipped out the old, yellowing map and lit a torch. "It's so hard to get your bearings when you can't see anything."

He stood up straight and held the map in front of his face, then he lowered it, then he raised it again, then he turned it one way and then the other. And then he did this several more times.

"I need a wee now," said Syeeda.

"Go in that carriage," said Ffion. "No-one'll notice."

"I can't wee in there! Somebody lives in there!" Syeeda hissed.

"It hasn't stopped *them*!"

"I'll find somewhere else. Roz, do you need to go?"

"No. Bladder of iron."

"Back in a mo," said Syeeda. And off she went.

"Any joy?" Rosalind asked Rich.

"Yeah. I'm pretty sure that it's..." With the beam of light from his torch, he followed the curve of the crescent-shaped platform. "...there."

Three circles of light came to rest upon the spot Rich had identified. The platform, at its outermost curve, met a red-bricked wall that projected upwards and over their heads like an ocean wave at the point of breaking.

"But there's nothing there," said Ffion. "Just a wall."

"Well, that's where the map says it is," said Rich.

"Better go take a look, then," said Rosalind.

"Don't go anywhere without me!" a voice yelled out from somewhere in the blackness.

"Relax, Syd," Ffion called back. "We're only going along the platform a bit!"

"Oh! Okay!"

Rich ran his hand over the brickwork. "I don't get it. I'm sure it said it's here."

"So what form does this entrance take?" Rosalind asked. "Is it a door? Is it a tunnel?"

"Well, that's just it," replied Rich. "I don't actually know."

"Does this mean we can go home?" a hopeful Ffion asked.

Rosalind let out a little chuckle. "Not wishful thinking at all, there."

Ffion didn't reply. However, she did jump when she heard the clang of metal on metal from somewhere in the gloom followed by an "Ow!"

"Shit myself then, mun," she said.

"Soz," said Syeeda, who had still yet to reappear.

"Such a sincere and heartfelt apology," said Rosalind.

Noisily, Syeeda clambered back up onto the platform.

"Is that better?" asked Ffion, as if she were addressing a toddler.

"Yeah, In fact, I'd probably put that in the top three wees I've ever had in my life."

"Must have been good," said Ffion. Then her stomach rumbled. "That's me again. Sorry."

"Good lord," said Roz. "That sounded like an old ZX Spectrum loading up."

"What's a ZX Spectrum?" asked Syeeda.

"I'll explain later."

"Girls," said Rich, interrupting, "can you all look around to see if you can find any kind of seam or something. There should be a doorway here or a tunnel or some sort of way in."

"Maybe there's a secret entrance," grinned Ffion, "like in Indiana Jones."

"Never ceased to amaze me how all those ancient civilisations could build contraptions that would still work after gathering dust for centuries and without any kind of power source," said Rosalind.

"Bloody hell, Roz, mun," exclaimed Ffion. "They're just films. Trust you."

"Can't help it. Just the way my mind works."

"Maybe the entrance has been bricked up," said Syeeda.

"Yeah," said Ffion, eyes widening with excitement. "The entrance must be behind that wall. Let's try lobbing something at it."

Confident that things were once again about to get interesting, Rich switched the camera on and pressed record.

"Have a look around for something heavy," Rosalind said. "There must be something around here we can use."

Syeeda stepped onto the driver plate of one of the engines parked next to the platform. "There's probably something in one of these trains," she said.

There came the shrill sound of metal meeting stone. "Someone give me a hand with this," said Rosalind. She was, with some difficulty, dragging a boiler plate along the platform.

"Yeah, that should do it," said Ffion as she trotted over to help.

"Ready," said Rosalind as Syeeda joined them. "One, two, three, now."

Huffing and puffing, the three explorers hoisted the cold, heavy, metal disc to waist-height and shuffled over to the wall.

"A hand would be nice, Rich," wheezed Ffion.

"Sorry. Filming."

"Right then," said Rosalind, having obviously assumed command. "Three swings and we let it go. Right?"

"Uh huh."

"Yep."

"Here we go. One..."

In a shallow arc, the boiler plate swung out and back toward the wall.

"Two..."

Momentum building, the boiler plate swung outwards and then inwards again.

"Three..."

This time the boiler plate assumed an almost vertical position on its outward swing, before arcing back toward the wall and crashing with an almighty clang on the floor. In their pools of light, Rosalind, Syeeda and Ffion all looked at each other blankly before bursting out laughing.

"That was pathetic!" gasped Syeeda.

"God, we're so rubbish!" Ffion agreed between fits of laughter.

Rosalind was crouched over in hysterics. "Think we'd better go back to the drawing board," she cried.

Rich did not crack a smile. Instead, he just carried on filming from the shadows like a silent ghost.

"Come on," said Ffion, still laughing. "Let's find something else."

"Yeah. Something a bit lighter," Syeeda added.

"Try wrenching one of those levers off the train," said Rich from behind the camera.

"He speaks!" exclaimed Rosalind.

"What levers?" asked Ffion.

"From the driver's carriage. Is it a brake lever? Either way it looks big and heavy."

Ffion stepped onto the driver plate of the nearest engine. "Oi, Syd. Gissa hand." Ffion and Syeeda gripped the lever and heaved it back. There was no give whatsoever.

"Again," wheezed Ffion.Straining every muscle and sinew, arms trembling with effort, they again heaved back on the lever, but still with no joy.

"Jesus Christ," panted Ffion. "We're never going to get that off."

Rosalind got down onto her hands and knees and aimed her head torch at the lever connection on the floor. "Maybe we could unscrew it," she said. "Has anybody got a coin?"

"Fuck me," said Ffion. "We're going to be here all night."

A small round disc of light suddenly appeared in the gloom. "Actually," said Rich, "it's still only eleven-fifteen. Not even the afternoon yet."

"Oh, that's alright then," Ffion conceded.

"Coin? Anyone?"

"Not me," said Syeeda. "I never carry cash."

"Don't tell me," said Rosalind. "You've got an app."

"Yep," Ffion confirmed. "She pays by pointing her phone at things. Here's a quid, Roz, but I want it back."

Rosalind took it from her. "Nope. Too Big. Got twenty pence?"

"Oh, Jesus eff, mun! Here you go."

"Aha. That's more like it."

After a moment or two of clanking noises, the lever fell away from its holding and clattered onto the footplate.

"Right then," said Rosalind, wielding it like a club and taking aim at the wall. "Let's give this a go."

"Ooh, can I do it?" asked a visibly excited Ffion. "I loves breaking things, me."

"Oh, go on then," said Rosalind as she handed over the tool. "Just be careful."

Ffion was initially surprised by how heavy the lever was, but she swung it out and held it in position ready to strike, like a pro baseball player.

"Are you filming, Rich?" she asked.

"Yep. Go for it."

Rosalind and Syeeda narrowed their eyes in readiness for the immense noise.

"One, two, three," said Ffion, and she swung the lever as hard as she could.

The metal-on-brick clang hit like an explosion, sending sparks flying. The brickwork gave way, sending debris tumbling around Ffion's feet. She danced backwards out of the way.

"Nice one," nodded Syeeda.

"I never knew you had it in you," said Rosalind.

Ffion dropped the lever and struck a bodybuilder pose,

flexing her biceps. "Strong as an ox, me," she beamed.

Still holding the camera in front of his face, Rich began to walk slowly toward the collapsed wall. Rosalind, Syeeda and Ffion fell silent as he focused in on what had been exposed.

"It's a door!" gasped Rosalind.

"That's a door?" asked a perplexed Syeeda. "But it's huge!"

"Looks like it's made of steel," said Ffion, tapping it.

The circles of light from their head torches shimmered across the surface of this monstrous circular door. In its centre was a huge, heavy wheel, like those found on the bridges of old sailing ships.

"What's that on the floor?" asked Syeeda.

All beams were now focussed on the floor. In front of the door and implanted into the ground was a brass seal with a diameter of about a metre.

"There's words on it," said Ffion. "But I can't make them out."

Rosalind put a knee to the ground and brushed some of the dirt away. In the centre of the seal was a Christian cross, and at each point of the cross was a name. She read them out: "Iesus. Nazarenus. Rex. Iudaerum."

"I take it those i's are supposed to be j's," said Syeeda.

"God, that's creeping me out, that is," said Ffion.

"Same," said Syeeda.

"What do you think it means, Roz?" Ffion asked.

"I don't know. Maybe it's a blessing of some sort. You know, like the grounds of a church are supposedly hallowed. It wouldn't surprise me if this ground had been blessed at some point in time."

"Why?" Syeeda asked, genuinely flummoxed.

"People probably died here. Building this place and working here must have been very dangerous. This could very well be the last resting place of quite a few people."

"Yeah. Creeeepy," said Syeeda, nodding her head and looking around suspiciously.

Rich suddenly became aware of battery life draining away. "Right. Shall we get on then?" he said chirpily from behind the camera. "Roz, you'd better say something."

"Right. Yes," said Rosalind, pulling herself together and standing up. She positioned herself in front of the mighty steel door and faced the camera. Syeeda and Ffion joined her on either side.

"Okay. Rolling," said Rich.

"Um...in this abandoned service point which apparently dates from the Victorian era, we have uncovered this door. The fact that it had been bricked up, along with its sheer size, indicates that whatever lies behind it was never meant to be found."

Good, good, thought Rich.

"We're going to try opening it. Ladies, shall we?"

Each taking a point, Rosalind, Syeeda and Ffion assumed strong stances around the wheel and prepared to use force.

"Towards me," said Rosalind. "GO!"

Rosalind pulled and Syeeda and Ffion pushed, but the wheel would not give.

"Try the other way," wheezed Rosalind.

Rosalind pushed and Syeeda and Ffion pulled, but the result was the same.

"It's no good," panted Ffion. "It won't budge!"

"Hang on a minute," snapped Syeeda. "There's a keyhole here. Rich, have you got a key for this?"

"Yeah, cos if not it looks like we're all going home," said Ffion, with hope flashing in her eyes.

So this is where the key comes into it, thought Rich. "Yes. The old man gave me a key! Hang on."

"What old man?"

"Explain later." He would never get the chance.

He slipped the pack from his back, unzipped a side pocket, and produced from it a large brass key. Reverentially, cupping it in both hands, he slowly walked over to Rosalind and offered it to her. With due sense of ceremony, Rosalind took the key from Rich as Syeeda and Ffion looked on silently. With the backpack between his feet on the floor, Rich once again raised the video camera to his face.

"Rolling," he said, and then held his breath.

Rosalind held the key up before her and looked to camera. "I have here an old brass key that we think may be the one for this mysterious door. Let's give it a try."

Rich zoomed in as Rosalind inserted the key into the hole. The lock was stiff and required some force, but it turned. From behind the door came a series of large metallic clangs, as if some great mechanism had been set in motion. Syeeda and Ffion both took a step back.

*...contraptions that would still work after gathering dust for centuries without any kind of power source...*The words that she had spoken only a few moments ago sprung back into Rosalind's mind.

"It appeared to work," said Rosalind, addressing the camera. "Let's try the wheel again. Towards me. Ready?"

Again, Rosalind pulled, and her friends pushed. She could feel the resistance in the mechanism begin to give way, and the wheel started to turn. Suddenly, the wheel gave, and the mighty door began to open. Upon the breaking of its seal, a great, stale sigh was released into the dusty air. And then it swung fully open, causing the three women to skip backwards out of the way.

"God, that was a bit spooky." Ffion whispered with a shiver.

"Yeah. Was a bit," Syeeda said.

Rosalind realised that the hairs on the back of her neck were now standing to attention. She raised her right leg and moved to step over the threshold. She glanced back to Syeeda and Ffion.

"Well, here goes..." she said.

Suddenly, Rich barged past her, almost knocking her off her feet.

"Oi! Watch it!" Rosalind snapped.

"Sorry. Want to film you entering from the inside."

"He's very demanding when he's got his director's hat on, isn't he?" quipped Syeeda.

"Sorry," Rich mumbled again. He'd overstepped the mark and he knew it. "This is an important moment – the discovery of the deep level – so I just wanted it to be perfect."

"That's okay, Rich," Rosalind sighed.

From beyond the threshold, Rich issued his instructions. "Right then. Roz. You step in first, and then Fee and Syd. You have a bit of a look round, and then, Roz, you address the camera."

"What do you want me to say?"

"This is a pretty momentous occasion. You've just taken your first step into a place that's been walled up since the Victorian era. It needs to be something that captures the gravitas of such an important moment."

"Right. I understand."

"Okay. Ready when you are."

Rosalind, Syeeda and Ffion all exchanged a look, and then Rosalind entered the unknown.

Rich watched the ghostly grey action unfold on his viewfinder:

Here, in these unfathomed depths, three beams of light suddenly cut through the darkness. A figure appears in the circular entranceway. It is Roz, the expedition's leader. Slowly, tentatively, she steps over the threshold and enters. She casts a pool of light around her as she explores this strange new space. Two more figures appear. Gingerly, they too take their first steps into this forbidden place. What will they find? Nobody knows. This place was built in secret and was never meant to be discovered. The three brave explorers come together, forming a tight unit. Rosalind turns to the camera to address us, the viewers, her silent companions on this strange adventure. The profundity of this discovery weighs heavily on all present. What will she say? How can mere words express such deep, reverential feelings.

Finally, she speaks..

"Oh, goody. Another bloody tunnel."

"Oh, Roz! For goodness sake!" Rich was not happy.

"Actually, this is more like a passage than a tunnel," Ffion pointed out.

"Yeah, it is," said Syeeda. "Look, it goes curving off in

both directions."

"Like a giant circle," Ffion continued.

"We'll have to do that again," Rich said.

"We're not doing it again," Rosalind stated flatly as she rolled her eyes. "You'll just have to use what you've got."

"Yeah. Let's just get on with it," huffed Ffion.

Impatience was clearly setting in so Rich relented.

"Smells worse than a rugby player's jockstrap in here," Ffion pointed out.

"You should know," Syeeda laughed. "But, yeah. Smells like something's died."

"Grounds really wet and all," Ffion pointed out.

Syeeda turned and started back towards the entrance. "Won't be a mo," she said as her feet slip-slapped through the puddles. When there, she pulled the big brass key from the door and pocketed it.

Don't want to lose this, she thought.

Chapter Six

Walking carefully backwards, Rich continued to film as his three friends tentatively made their way towards him. The passageway was fairly narrow and quite low, and Rosalind, Syeeda and Ffion huddled together.

"Don't shine your head torches into the camera," Rich instructed.

"The ground's very slippery," Rosalind quietly remarked.

"I know," whispered Ffion. "I'm going to go arse over tit any minute now."

"Such a classy lady," said Syeeda.

"That's me," said Ffion proudly.

"Walls are slimy too," Syeeda added.

"Any idea what we're looking for, Rich?" Rosalind asked.

"Yes and no," he replied. "All I've seen of the deep level is a map and some architectural plans. The layout itself is pretty straightforward, but the access points are like mazes. Which was deliberate, I suspect. So we're kind of in unknown territory here. That's why it's very important to remember which way we came down so that we can find our way back up."

"Hear that, ladies," Rosalind said, "On no account go wandering off on your own. No matter what, we have to stick together from here on in."

"I'm not going sodding anywhere," said Ffion.

"Same," said Syeeda. "It's far too scary."

"And another thing," Rich continued. "When we're down there, we have to stick to the train tracks. Don't go wandering off into any of the service tunnels because they were like mazes too. You disappear into one of them, chances are you ain't gonna come back."

Rosalind realised how cold it was and zipped her jacket up to the top, just under her chin. Then she suddenly stopped, and her friends with her.

"What's going on?" asked Syeeda.

"Sh. Listen," whispered Rosalind. There was nothing to be heard. "Eerie, isn't it?"

"Hm," said either Syeeda or Ffion. Rosalind could not tell which.

"I thought it was quiet before, but this is different. Like a vacuum. Like being in space. Outer space."

"Like we'd know."

That was definitely Fee, thought Rosalind.

They could feel what she meant. The air that they were breathing, having been filtered through hundreds of feet of concrete, rock and soil felt still and lifeless.

"Come on. Let's keep moving." Cautiously, Rosalind Syeeda and Ffion continued on.

On the deathly grey viewfinder, Rich saw emerging into shot the gaping mouth of a semi-circular doorway. "Head's up," he said. "This could be it."

There was a clang.

"What was that?" Ffion asked.

"I just hit my head on something," said Rich.

The three circles of light all focussed in on an ornate metal arm extending from the wall. It was holding a large brass gas lamp that had for decades remained unlit..

"There's another one here," said Rich.

There were two gas lamps, one either side of the tunnel entrance.

"Ooh. What have we here?" Rosalind asked no one in particular.

Around the curve of this new entrance was an ornately carved plaque, glistening in milky-yellow.

Rosalind ran a hand over it. "It feels cold," she said.

"Do you think it's gold?" asked an excited Ffion.

"No. It's brass, I reckon."

"What's it say?"

"Iesus. Nazarenus. Rex. Iudaerum. Same as back there."

"Can you see what's down there?" Syeeda asked.

Rosalind, Syeeda and Ffion aimed their head torches into the tunnel. A flight of steps plummeted downwards into the depths. Rich's heart quickened and he felt his stomach tighten. *So close now*, he thought.

"That's weird," whispered Syeeda. "It's like our torches are just pointing at nothing."

"Yeah," Ffion breathed. "It's just black down there."

"It's like the light is being swallowed up by the darkness," said Rosalind to the camera.

"Maybe the walls are actually black," Ffion suggested. "What's the German for darkness, Syd?"

"Dunkelheit,"

"Dunkelheit. Dunkelheit," Ffion repeated.

"It's really odd," Rosalind added. "I've never seen anything like it."

"Well, shall we then?" said Rich from behind the camera.

But Rosalind hesitated. "As the passageway we're in now seems to be one big circle," she began, "perhaps we should follow it all the way around. You never know what else we might find."

"I think we should just go straight down," said Rich. "This is what we've been looking for."

"I don't know," said Rosalind. "I can't help thinking that it's a little odd that there'd be a really long circular passage up here with just one tunnel down to the deep level in it. It doesn't make sense. I think we should just make sure that we're not missing anything."

Syeeda's and Ffion's eyes darted to Rich. He looked torn.

"We-e-e-ell. I suppose. Maybe."

"So we're carrying on?" Ffion asked.

"We're carrying on," Rich confirmed. And a few minutes later they found an identical tunnel entrance. And a few minutes after that another one.

"Well, there's tunnel entrances right the way around here, so which one are we going to go down, Rich?" Ffion asked. She was growing impatient.

"Better make it this one, I suppose," he replied. "As long

65

as we remember, when we come back out, to turn left."

"Yep," said Rosalind. "And then the exit back out to the service point will be on our right."

"Mm hm. Okay, are we ready?"

"After you," said Syeeda and Ffion in unison.

"I can't go first," said Rich. "I've got to follow you guys."

"I'll go first," said Rosalind with a roll of the eyes. "Ready, Rich?"

"Ready."

"Okay. This is it," said Rosalind to camera. "This is the tunnel that's going to lead us down to the deep level. I have no idea what's waiting for us down there. The tunnel is completely black so I'm a little bit scared but very excited at the same time."

Rich watched the plumes of breath escaping Rosalind's mouth as she spoke, evaporating into the icy-cold air.

"Okay. Here we go." Rosalind inhaled deeply and stepped into the tunnel. Syeeda and Ffion followed close behind, still clutching each other tightly. Rich, as stony-faced as ever, brought up the rear.

"Ooh. There's a handrail," said Syeeda.

"Fuck me, that's cold," Ffion gasped.

"It's brass again," said Rosalind.

"Well, whatever it is," said Syeeda, "it was very nice of them to think of us and put it here."

"Those Victorians really did love their brass, didn't they?" said Ffion.

"Sure did," Syeeda agreed.

"They were rather partial to séances too, from what I understand," said Rosalind.

"Ooh, don't," said Ffion. "That sort of thing terrifies me."

"These steps are very slippery," said Syeeda, changing the subject.

"Mm," agreed Ffion.

"I can't see all the way to the bottom so there's no way of knowing how far down these steps go," said Rosalind.

"Maybe we're just going to keep going down forever," Ffion offered.

"It's a lovely thought," said Syeeda drily. "But let's hope not."

"Look at this," Rosalind said. Her hand swept over the surface of the wall to her right. It glistened with frost. "The wall's frozen."

"That's amazing," breathed Ffion. "I didn't think it was *this* cold."

"And the walls aren't actually black, either. I don't like this," Syeeda moaned.

"It's alright," Rosalind soothed. "Won't be long now. This tunnel can't go on forever."

Through his viewfinder, all Rich could see in the grainy grey murkiness were the backs of the heads of his three friends, bobbing around in the gloom.

Rosalind gasped and nearly stumbled. "Ooh! Bloody hell. Guess this is it then."

She had emerged from the tunnel onto level ground. Syeeda and Ffion bumped into the back of her. They had arrived.

BOOK TWO:

DEEP LEVEL

Chapter One

"Make way. Make way," said Rich as he squeezed his way past Syeeda and Ffion and onto the platform. As always, his poker face was giving away nothing, but inside his heart was pounding and his mind was racing. He was finally here. He had made it.

With his fingers trembling and an internal cash register ringing in his ears, he fumbled around with the video camera. Viewing the scene in murky grey, he panned from left to right and from down to up. This subterranean otherworld in which the four friends now found themselves could not be described as a station so much as a frozen grotto. The walls, slathered with inches of slippery-slimy lichen, glistened and sparkled in the torchlight.

Rosalind aimed her beam at the ground. "Look at this," she said. "The floor's tiled just like the passageway in my house. That's definitely Victorian."

"It's very ornate," Syeeda agreed.

"Yeah, I suppose," Ffion shrugged.

"Look up there," said Syeeda, aiming her head torch high above. "It's like a cave."

Above their heads, stalactites, formed over hundreds of thousands of years, extended their eerie milky fingers toward them. Ffion shuddered.

"It *is* a cave," said Rosalind. "When you think about it, this wasn't technically a station. It was for the private use of a handful of extremely rich people and was never meant for the public."

"Are those more gas lamps over there?" asked Ffion.

"Looks like it," Rosalind answered.

Protruding from the rough, stone wall opposite, was a

rusted, cobwebbed old gas lamp, held aloft by an ornate iron holding. Following the line of the train tracks Rosalind espied another lamp about six metres further on, and six metres further on from that another one.

"The line was illuminated by gas lamps back in the day," she said. "Interesting."

"And check out behind," said Syeeda.

There were three tunnel entrances in the rock.

"Jesus Christ!" Ffion exclaimed. "No one forget which one we just came out of, for god's sake."

They had just emerged from the one on the far right.

"So they all must go back up to the circular passageway at the top," said Rosalind. "We came down the third tunnel up there, and came out of the third tunnel down here."

"Weird that there'd be so many tunnels when there were only a few people using this," Syeeda observed.

"So what now, Rich?" asked Ffion. "Are we done? Can we go home? I want my Harvester."

"What? No way," Rich blurted out as a million and one financial calculations whizzed through his head. "This is why we're here, to document this. This is the deep level. We've made it. These tunnels haven't seen any life since the god knows when. It's not enough to just find ourselves in one station. We've got to follow those tracks and find another. To prove that there's a network."

"So is that a no, then?" asked Syeeda, and everyone laughed. Everyone, that is, except for Rich.

"So, Rich," said Rosalind. "Are you planning on exploring all the tunnels down here?"

"Yes, but that's probably going to take me a few weeks."

"So does that mean you're going to want us to come back?" Ffion cautiously asked. She couldn't decide whether to hope for a yes or a no.

"Yes," Rich replied. "Filming today, full-on exploring later, and then some more filming at a later date. What I'll do is find all the really interesting locations and the easiest ways to get to them and then we can all come back. What do you think?"

Rosalind and Syeeda agreed. Ffion pulled the subject back to the here and now. "Can we get a shift on then, is it or what?" she moaned. "Time's getting on."

"We need to do a bit for the camera first," said Rich. "This is a momentous occasion. We're making history here. Rosalind?"

"Righto."

Rosalind took her place in front of the camera and her two friends theirs at her sides.

"Well, after more than seventy years," she began, "the mysterious deep level has finally been revealed. This is where, over a hundred and fifty years ago, the superrich of the Victorian era constructed themselves a secret underground train network. And then, back in the days of the Second World War, the rich and powerful of that era took shelter here from the bombs of the Luftwaffe. And here it is..."

Rich panned around with the camera, following the line of the train tracks that swept from his left to his right, taking in the row of gas lamps on the wall opposite, before finally resting on the deathly black tunnel mouth into which the tracks disappeared.

"Now, this space that we're in is not much to look at," Rosalind continued. "The floor is tiled in a Victorian fashion, but other than that there doesn't appear to be any decoration down here whatsoever. This wasn't a working station, it was specifically built for private use, and it looks like it was all just carved out of the rock. There's gas lamps on the wall opposite there, but that's about it. They were obviously put there to illuminate the line."

Rich zoomed in on one of the gas lamps.

"Now, we're going to follow the train tracks through that tunnel there and see what we can find."

"After you," said Syeeda and Ffion in unison.

Rosalind sighed and rolled her eyes at the camera. Rich gave a little smirk. Then Rosalind turned and clambered down from the platform and onto the train tracks. Arms linked, Syeeda and Ffion followed. They entered the tunnel and a curtain of blackness closed in upon them.

For a good while, nobody spoke. As it had in the tunnels far above, the silence had become oppressive and no one wanted to be the first to test its brittleness. At first they all stepped cautiously along, hugging the side of the wall. But, unlike the tunnels above, this one did not have a deep wide groove for the trains that had ran through it. It was flat, and so eventually they all fanned out a little, stepping lightly over the tracks.

The cold was starting to eat its way into Rosalind's bones. She shuddered slightly and dug her hands deep into her pockets. Then she felt an arm work its way through the crook of her own, and Ffion snuggled in beside her. A body pressed in close on her opposite side. It was Syeeda. The three of them were now linked, arm in arm in arm, and in this way, quietly and with quiet confidence, they continued forward.

Seeing this, Rich raised the camera viewfinder to his eye and hit record. This would be a lovely moment, he knew, in his documentary. And in realising this, he suddenly felt himself growing colder still. Not through anydrop in temperature, but through the realisation that this was something that was missing from his life. This non-intimate intimacy. This warm, bodily brand of friendship. This comfortable closeness.

Eventually Ffion caved in and spoke first. "I think my battery's running out."

"I've got spare batteries for everyone in my backpack," Rich said.

"I just saw it flickering."

"Like I said..."

"Don't suppose you've got any energy bars in there, have you, Rich?" asked Syeeda.

"'Fraid not."

"I don't even know what an energy bar is," said Ffion. "What *is* an energy bar?"

Rich and Syeeda competed to say it first. "It's a bar that gives you energy."

"Ha ha."

Rosalind stopped suddenly. "Ssh."

"Whassup, Roz," Ffion whispered.

"I thought I heard something," Rosalind replied. "From up ahead." She felt Syeeda and Ffion cuddle in tight.

"What did it sound like?" Syeeda quietly asked, her freezing breath wafting into the air like a ghost.

Rosalind turned to her gravely. "Just kidding," she beamed.

"Aw, Roz, mun!" Ffion bellowed. "I fucking shit myself then!"

Rich almost cracked a smile from behind his video camera.

Laughing, Rosalind started forward again, dragging her friends along with her.

"Rich," said Ffion after a few more minutes of silence. "My torch is flickering again."

"We'll change the batteries when we get to the next station. Or cavern. Or whatever."

"Okay."

Around them, the air pressure seemed to change, and they could sense that they were no longer in the tunnel.

"Whoah," Ffion exclaimed. "This place is huge!"

"Incredible!" breathed Rosalind.

Rich's heart thumped hard and his hot blood throbbed through the veins in his ears. All his little reveries about this expedition were coming true. Slowly, he surveyed the vast, empty space through the fuzzy grey filter of the camera viewfinder. As he slowly panned across, taking in the curving tracks and the gas lamps on the wall, there was a blinding flash of light.

"What the fuck?" he gasped.

Blinking, Rosalind said, "Syd. Was that you?"

"Yeah. Just wanted to get a selfie. Soz."

"Bloody hell, Syd, mun," said Ffion. "I can't see nothing here!"

"I can't see *anything* here," said Syeeda, correcting her.

"Cheeky. For that I'm not letting you come to Harvester with me."

"You weren't anyway!"

"Rich," said Rosalind, nodding towards something in the blackness. "Have you seen that?"

Lowering his camera, Rich followed her beam of light. It was illuminating three tunnel entrances, each with stairs ascending.

"Three stairways on the platform. Just like the last cavern."

"Don't tell me we're going to go up one of them," said Ffion, her voice loaded with hesitation.

"We'll have to," he said. "I just want to test a theory."

"What theory?" Rosalind asked.

"That what's up those stairs is exactly the same as what was up those other stairs," replied Rich.

"Isn't that all the more reason why we shouldn't go up them," Syeeda pointed out. "I mean, if all these tunnels and stairways and everything are exactly the same, aren't we just going to get lost?"

"All we're going to do," said Rich, "is go to the top of one of those flights of stairs and see what's up there. Once we've had a look, we're going to come back down and then find our back and call it a day."

"Woohoo! Harvester here we come!" cheered Ffion.

"Yay," said Syeeda lazily.

Inside, Rosalind was as relived as her friends. As much as she was enjoying the experience of exploring secret underground stations that had lain dormant for decades, she was looking forward to once again standing in the frosty daylight and breathing the cool, fresh air. She hadn't shown it, but the darkness was starting to close in on her. She was feeling claustrophobic and anxious.

"We just need to remember," said Rich, "that when we come back down, it's left at the bottom, through the tunnel and then the stairway on the right to take us back up. Then it's left at the top of that and that'll lead us back to the service point, and from there everything's mapped."

"Yeah. And going back never takes as long as getting there. Isn't that right?" chirped Ffion.

"More wishful thinking," grinned Syeeda.

"Shuddup."

"Okay, piece to camera please, Roz," said Rich with a certain air of authority.

"Bloody 'ell," Ffion remarked. "Get him!"

"I said please," Rich sheepishly added.

"Oh, alright then," said Rosalind. "Are you ready?"

"Ready."

Without even thinking, Syeeda and Ffion took their places beside Rosalind. This had become a routine for them now.

"Here in the deep level, we've discovered another station, and another set of stairways leading upwards..."

"Cut! Syd, what are you doing?"

Syeeda, who had been holding two fingers up behind Rosalind's head and wiggling them about, laughed a guilty laugh.

"Soz." She grinned.

By the time he had lifted the camera back up and said 'Action', Rich had already decided that he would include that clip in a gag reel and post that too. *More content*!

"Here in the deep level," Rosalind began again, "we've found another station, much like the first. This one also has three stairways leading upwards to who knows where. Let's go and explore them." And off she walked, followed by her friends.

"Perfect," said Rich as he got in line behind them.

Much like the previous stairway, this one was lined with cold, brass handrails. They reached the top and found that it did indeed connect to a circular passageway at the top. But this time something was different.

"What the fuck is that?" Ffion gasped.

"Oh my days! Is that what I think it is," Syeeda squealed, hand over mouth.

"Oh, my god! It looks like a giant spider web," Rosalind breathed.

"Oh, don't say that," a panicky Ffion said as she clutched Rosalind's arm.

Rich barged past them with the camera. Through the

viewfinder he could see a large shapeless mass resting on the floor and clumped up against the wall. The pool of light from a head torch illuminated it for a moment. The mass was grey in colour.

"It looks more like dust," he said. "Like a big pile of dust."

"That's so weird," said Syeeda, her face scrunched up in bafflement. "What on earth is it?"

"Kick it, Roz," said Ffion.

"I'm not kicking it. You never know what might be underneath it."

"Well, I'm not kicking it either, before you ask," said Syeeda.

"Roz," said a feint voice at Rosalind's ear. It was Ffion. "You don't think there's a body under there do you?"

The mention of the word body caused a tightening in her stomach. "I don't know," she whispered. "I hope not."

"I really, really don't like this," said Syeeda. She was trembling now from fear as much as cold. "I think we should go now."

"Rich, you're not really gonna come back here on your own, are you, like you said?" a very nervous Ffion asked.

"No, I don't think so," he said in a small, timid voice. "I'll...er...come back with other people. I don't know. Like the authorities or something, I suppose. It's going to take a professional team to map all this. And see what that is." He nodded towards the amorphous lump on the floor.

"So are we done here?" asked Roz, hardly daring to disturb the blackness by raising her voice above a whisper.

"Yes, we're done," said Rich. "Let's go."

"Well thank fuck for that," said Ffion in hushed tones. "Roz. You first."

With the mysterious mass behind them, slowly, gingerly, they crept back down the stairway, one step at a time. As they neared the bottom, they turned their head torches towards the end of the tunnel and the platform beyond, and then all sense of reality left them.

Chapter Two

Individually, they all became suddenly aware of a change in the atmosphere, as if the air had become electromagnetically charged. Pulses quickened, throats tightened, hairs prickled. One by one, each inextricably knowing that something was about to happen, Rosalind, Syeeda and Ffion fixed their head torches onto the platform at the end of the tunnel and waited.

Behind them, Rich could feel it too, the sense that they were not alone down here. He wanted to raise his eyes, but he could not bring himself to, despite them still being shielded by his nightvision goggles. He was afraid, and so he continued to observe the scene via the filter of his viewfinder.

The silenced pierced them. Everything was frozen, even time. Breathing was suspended, and the ghosts of breaths already exhaled drifted away. And then it came.

Into the collective pool of light, an engine rolled. It was an engine of the type that they had seen at the service point; a swollen, rusted iron boiler mounted on large spindly wheels with a stovepipe protruding from the top.

Slowly, the vessel moved along the platform's edge and came to a halt. And it did so completely silently and without letting loose a single wisp of steam. The alien nature of the arrival of this vehicle, without the accompanying whistles, hisses and clouds of water vapour, sent approximately one million thoughts racing through the minds of the four friends within the space of one single nanosecond; how is this possible? Is it a trick? Has it been modified?Is it electric? Who else is down here? Where's the driver?

The engine stayed silent and motionless at the platform edge, as if lying in wait. Rosalind, Syeeda and Ffion stood tightly together, stiff and straight, hands gripping arms, breathless and still, just like the engine itself.

They expected to hear a voice –someone calling out a hello, perhaps – but none came.

Rich still hadn't looked up. Open-mouthed and frightened, he had watched the scene unfold in fuzzy monochrome. Then, finally, something moved. He saw the indistinct image of Ffion lean into the hazy figure of Rosalind.

"Roz. What are we going to do?"

Eyes wide, not daring to look anywhere but forward lest the wandering pool of light capture something else that should not be, Rosalind, with great effort, took a step forward. And, as if a single mass, her two friends moved with her.

The beams from the head torches remained fixed on the engine. They all thought, without knowing that the thought had been shared by the others, that if the engine was left in darkness for just one single second, it would disappear. And then what? Running? Screaming?

Rosalind, Syeeda and Ffion reached the point where the stairway ended and the platform began. Silently, taking just one tentative step at a time, they continued to edge their way forward. There was no sign of anyone else. No hint of movement. No sign of life.

Rosalind tried to swallow but couldn't. Her throat was as arid as a desert. Her body shivered from the cold and the fear. As terrified as she was, she was also desperate to know if this object in front of her was real, tangible, because the alternative was far too terrible to contemplate. Such thoughts led to a dark chasm, a place where the ground beneath ones feet no longer existed. To a place where if one thing was not real, then neither was the next, nor the next. So she reached out a hand towards the great iron boiler, knowing that if her hand rested on solid, cold metal, then the vehicle was real, and that meant that there was a reason for it being here, an explanation.

With their pupils dilated to maximum capacity, black and round, Syeeda and Ffion watched breathlessly as Rosalind's hand inched closer and closer to the engine – and then the screams began.

The following eight seconds of Ffion's life consisted of rapid movement, confusion, piercing shrieks, a flickering pool of light, a feeling of weightlessness, a terrific thump as something cold and metallic connected with her face, the taste of blood in her mouth and then nothing.

Ffion! She just disappeared! The thought flashed through Syeeda's mind in an nth of a second and then vanished as another scream filled the cavern – *No! No oh god no*! There to her right, a tunnel, a tunnel out of here. She sprinted for it and stumbled on the first step. Something sharp drove into her shin and she yelled, swore. With her eyes watering from the pain, she scrambled to her feet and ran up the steps, away from the screaming and the engine.

"ROZ," she screamed in desperation. "ROZ! WHERE ARE YOU?"

Where was that coming from? Rosalind heard her name echoing through the cold blackness. It seemed to ricochet into her ears from every direction. The sound of her name blended with the screams from the tunnel. Rich's screams. She was frozen to the spot. Where was Fee? She had just vanished! But Syd was still calling for her.

"SYD! WHERE ARE YOU? SYYYYD!"

Over her own yelling and panting and the echoes of Rich's screams, Syeeda could not discern Rosalind's cries. And now she was here, back in the long circular passageway at the top of the tunnel. She turned left and ran a few paces before putting her back up against the wall. In this position, nothing could come up behind her. No cold, spindly hands could grasp her and pull her back down into the deep level. But from here, in this passageway, she could hear Rich, and he was pleading for his life.

"OH GOD! PLEASE, NO! PLEASE PLEASEPLEASE! OH GOD, NOOOOOOOOO!"

Rosalind felt a terror beyond anything that her dark, witching-hour imagination had ever visited upon her. She had stopped breathing, she was poised in readiness to flee, and every single atom in her body was now focused on the sound of Rich's pleas.

"N O O O O O O O O ! O H   G O D ,   P L E A S E !
NOOOOOOOOOO!"

Her jaw quivering and her pupils wide with fright, she
forced her head, and the pool of light that it projected,
towards the tunnel to where Rich had fled.

"PLEEEAAASE PLEEEAAASE PLEEEAAASE!"

He was crying now.

Something clattered in the darkness, as if an object of
plastic and metal had hit the cold, hard floor.

"RICH!" she screamed. The sound of her own voiced
shocked her. She hadn't decided to call his name, it had just
happened.

"RIIIIICH!" she screamed again.

And now there was nothing. Silence. What had happened?
Was he dead? She steeled herself and took a step towards the
black mouth of the tunnel, and then she felt a wind emerging
from the entranceway and with it the hot, pungent stench of
dead flesh. A low, guttural moaning sound began to rise and
so she turned and ran.

Chapter Three

Rich

He was sitting right where he said he would be, in a quiet corner of the pub, cradling a pint of beer. Rich looked around to see if anyone was watching. But then, why would they be?

He imagined that this had probably been a very nice pub once upon a time. Turning the grindstone of time back in his mind, he visualised it as it might have been during the days preceding the blitz; a sedate, subdued, smoky hidey hole, a quiet refuge from the toil and the grime outside, a place where working men with oily hands and worn faces could converse quietly over warm and weak ales.

But now it all just looked so...so corporate. So sterile. He looked back to the person he was here to meet. Mr Williams. He was thin and gaunt and wearing an old, worn cardigan and a flat cap. His pallor was grey, and this greyness seemed to infect his clothes and everything around him. Rich wondered if he had died years ago and just not realised it. The only splash of colour to be seen was on the football scarf that hung limply around his neck.

"Mister Williams?" said Rich, his voice little more than a nervous croak.

The old geezer looked up, and Rich, upon seeing the roadmap of veins around his nose and noticing how shaky his hands were, understood immediately what he wanted the money for.

"Pull up a chair," said the old man.

Rich took a seat but didn't say anything. He had rehearsed this moment over and over in his mind. He was going to be the one in charge. He was going to sit down and immediately take control of the conversation and get the info he wanted from the old man and then do the business and leave. Easy as. But now that he was actually here, all that meticulous planning and internal scriptwriting turned into mist and drifted out of his head, never to be seen or heard from again.

I'd make a rubbish spy, he thought.

"I was beginning to think I'd get through me whole life without anyone asking about it," Mr Williams began. "But no such luck, eh?"

"No. I suppose not. Do you want a drink?"

"Got one. Aren't you having one?"

"No. I don't drink."

"Oh." Mr William's head lowered slightly, and this tiny gesture awoke something in Rich.

Suddenly, unexpectedly, he felt a pang of empathy. Such occurrences were very unusual for Rich, and it had taken him somewhat by surprise. For just a moment, he had understood what it must be like to be this very old man who was sitting sadly in front of him. It was a crushing feeling, one of desperation and loneliness. He was so very old, and he'd probably been married once and had had to sit by and endure the agony of watching his wife pass on. He might have kissed her goodbye on her forehead after she had breathed her last. His kids were all grown up now and spread out all over the country with wives or husbands and children and probably even grandchildren of their own. Occasionally there would be a visit or a phone call, but over the years they had become less and less. One by one he had seen his friends fall by the wayside and die, and now he was the only one of his little childhood gang left. Everyone wanted to live a long life, but in this old man's eyes Rich saw that there was a point at which a life lived too long became a curse.

And now, some total stranger out of the blue had got in touch and had asked to meet up in his local to talk about a chapter from his past, so the old man had donned his cardie and his flat cap and, with weak knees and painful hips, had groaned his way to the pub in the hope of spending the evening drinking with and talking to a fellow human being.

And all this, Rich saw and understood from that one tiny gesture.

"I'll be right back," he said.

Mr Williams watched as this strange young man approached the young woman behind the bar. "Latte, please," he said, "and two packets of peanuts."

Rich returned to the little table and his companion for the evening. He slid a packet of peanuts over to him and said, "That's a West Ham scarf, isn't it?" He saw a flicker of life flash across the old man's pale eyes, and thus began a lengthy dissection of The Hammers' recent performances on the pitch.

By the time that particular topic of conversation had dried up, it had fallen dark outside, and the after-work drinkers had begun to drift away. Rich thought that now might be a good time to get down to business.

"So," he began. "About that map."

"Not just a map," said Mr Williams, and he reached down under his chair to retrieve a Tesco carrier. Protruding from it were about half-a-dozen sheets of fragile, yellowing paper, rolled into tight tubes. "There's also charts and plans. Like architectural plans and whatnot."

Rich's eyes widened. "Brilliant. Okay." The more information he had to work with the better.

"It was my old dad 'oo got these. He was an engineer, and after the war him and his boys had to go down to this underground train thing to seal it all up. It was Victorian, but it had been opened up for rich folk to take shelter in during the blitz."

"So why was it sealed up again afterwards? Do you know?"

"Dunno. My old dad never said. Wouldn't say. But something had happened down there, and people had died. So I dunno if maybe some of the tunnels collapsed or something and killed a few people. That could be a reason why they had to close it up. But it was strange, my dad said. Very strange."

Rich's heart quickened and he felt a pulse of excitement.

"Strange? How?"

"Just because of all the secrecy. My old dad said that government men were in charge of the whole thing. Powerful men. They oversaw everything, he said. It's like they wanted to make sure those tunnels were wiped clean and never found again."

"Curious."

"Yeah, and they had all the entrances bricked up so no one would find it. But it's all here in these plans."

Rich had to work hard to keep his excitement in check.

"My old dad said he wasn't supposed to have them. But he smuggled them out. Found them in a sort of library in the middle of it all. Anyway, he said as an engineer he'd never seen anything like the design on these tunnels. Not like the tube trains now but like a normal railway but underground. And by all the stations – stops, he called them, cos they weren't like normal stations – were three staircases all leading up but only one o' them would lead you to the way out. But there were no signs, see, cos it was all so secret. So only the rich folk that the underground were built for would know the way. And the people 'oo worked in there, o' course. And there were three 'ubs down there too."

"'Ubs?"

"Aye. 'Ubs."

Rich decided that he must have meant hubs.

"There were a library, like I said, and then there was the clubhouse which had a restaurant and a bar in it. And as well as them there was like an 'otel, where all the rich folk stayed when they was down there. It was like a city down there, he said."

"Incredible."

"Mmm. The Victorians made it all deliberately like a maze, but they were all bricked up or blown up, me old dad said."

"Blown up?"

"Yeah, I know. Bit dramatic, ain't it? All the entrances from ground level were blown up, me old dad said..."

Rich froze.

"...except for one."

Rich unfroze.

"Yeah, there's one entrance that's still accessible. Via the old Highgate train station, if I remember right."

"Highgate?"

"Yeah. Highgate. So, here it all is. All yours."

He passed the carrier bag over the table and Rich accepted it with a trembling hand. *This is it*, he thought. *Finally*!

The old man watched Rich peering into the bag. He cleared his throat. Rich looked up and stared at him blankly for a moment. Then, suddenly, he remembered.

"Ah, yes. Sorry. Here you are, as agreed." He passed an envelope full of money across the table and into a bony hand. Mr William's pocketed it without a word.

"Don't you want to count it?" Rich asked.

"Why? Do you think you might've given me too much?"

Money has a way of making certain people uncomfortable, and during the moment of awkward silence that followed, the old man fought a battle inside his head. On the one hand, he knew that the right thing to do would be to give this pleasant young man all the grim details about the weeks that his father had spent down in those tunnels. About how, as time went on, he had become more and more nervous, edgy and paranoid. About how, one by one, his fellow engineers had either disappeared or died in horrible circumstances. About how he had tried to abandon the job but had had a gun pulled on him by one of the government men. About how he had stolen the maps and plans so that one day he could prove what had happened, but that day had never come. About how his father had never been the same man again after his experiences underground, and would be forever fearful that he was being followed or watched. And lastly, about how he had died. Killed whilst attempting to defuse an unexploded bomb from the war. Or so the story had gone.

But on the other hand, he rationalised that whoever or whatever it was down in those tunnels that had picked off his father's colleagues one by one would certainly now be dead, wouldn't it? Of course it would. It had been sealed in for over seventy years. Nothing could survive in the cold and the dark for that long. Besides, there was something else at play. A thought that had niggled away in Mr Williams' mind and grown over the years and years and years; that the account of what had happened in the subterranean gloom given to him by his father a lifetime ago could not possibly have been true in the first place. Of course, he had believed everything he had been told at the time. It had been absorbed fully by his young, hungry mind. The tale had terrified him, but as he had grown older how could he not come to doubt such a fantastical story? He had lived all these decades without ever once seeing anything with his own two eyes that had made him question what was real and what was not. There had never been a single wisp of a ghost, a murmur of a voice from a dingy passageway, an icy cold touch in the dark corner of a scullery. As time had marched on, the fantastical had receded further and further into the distance until it had become nothing more than an unreliable shadow. And now, with this chasm of time stretching from horizon to horizon between his childhood and his inevitable death, Mr Williams had relegated the tale almost to insignificance. It had all but ceased to be. It had died of old age.

The old man sighed, relieved that the sceptical half of his mind had won out and that he was now spared the unenviable task of having to tell the young man all about this hokey unpleasant stuff. There was just one more thing to take care of, in that case.

"Before you go," he said, reaching into his pocket. "You won't be getting in without this." It was a big, brass key.

Rich emerged into the cool night air feeling alive and exhilarated. *Got 'em*, he thought. *Finally got 'em.* Every single thought sparking around in his leaping, jumping mind was now focused one single task; finding his way down to the deep level, filming it, getting recognition from it, and making money.

Out of all of these things, it was the making money part of it that he considered the most challenging. Actually selling the resulting footage. Making it palatable for the casual viewer. Finding the secret ingredient that would make it go viral. But he had come up with a plan, and all it required was the cooperation of three friends of his, Rosalind Brown, Syeeda Khan and Ffion Wyn Evans.

One more thing. He had promised to keep in touch with Mr Williams and meet up with him now and again for a drink and a chat. It never happened.

Chapter Four

Syeeda

Syeeda stopped running when she encountered another one of those piles of dust or cobwebs or whatever they were. She was back in the circular tunnel. She was sure she had run a complete circuit of it and had completely lost her bearings. Which stairway had originally led them down? Which one had she just run up? She had no idea. And where was the exit, the one that led to the service point where all those engines were and the carriage that someone was living in? There was no sign of it. Which meant that she must be in a different circular tunnel. Which in turn meant that she was lost.

"Oh fuck oh fuck oh fuck," she whispered.

Rich's screams had long since died away, and so had his begging and pleading. Was he dead? Oh god, please no. What the hell had happened to him? And where were her friends? Why couldn't she have been more in control? She hated the fact that when terror had struck she hadn't thought, she hadn't turned to her friends, she had just run. But then, hadn't everyone?

So now we're all scattered around in this black labyrinth with god knows what lurking around down here and absolutely no way of finding each other. Great.

The light from her head torch flickered. "Don't you dare," she rasped as she hit it with the flat of her hand. She realised she had just spoken out loud and put her hand over her mouth...and waited.

When the echoes from her voice had faded away and all that was left was cold, hard silence, her hunched shoulders and tightened stomach relaxed a little. She knew that she couldn't just wait here until someone came and found her – that was never going to happen – and she knew that she couldn't go calling out for her friends. Right now, that was definitely NOT an option. The only option that she did have, it seemed to her, was to pick one of these stairways at random, go down it, and see where she ended up.

A part of her hoped that she would find herself back on the platform where she had lost sight of Rosalind and Ffion, but a far larger part of her did not ever want to see that place again. Would that eerie train still be there? The silent train. Would she find Rich dead in the stairway he had fled into? Would she find the remains of her friends spread all over the platform? She ordered her mind to stop thinking such things.

Number one priority as of right now, to find Rosalind and Ffion. Priority number two: find Rich. Priority number three: get the hell out of here. With this sudden clarity of thought there came a swelling sense of resolution, of courage. Whatever had just happened, whatever was going on here, had to be faced. And so Syeeda picked a stairway and headed downwards, back into the stifling blackness.

She emerged onto a platform. It was either the same platform that she had just escaped from, or it was an identical one. Looking back, she again noted that there were three stairway entrances. She had just emerged from the middle one. She reasoned that when she had fled from the first platform and headed up the stairway, she had turned left at the top. So presumably she was now standing on the next platform along, so if she headed left again and followed the train tracks, she should, theoretically, end up back where she started. And then she'd be able to find her way back out, hopefully with her friends in tow.

She considered calling to them again but decided against it. She hopped down from the platform, her feet landing between the train tracks, and faced the gaping hole of the tunnel. Every atom in her body screamed out; *don't go in the tunnel, don't go in the tunnel*. But there was no choice.

How did this happen? She thought. *How did I end up*

here? She could not wait for the day when this nightmare had become just a memory. *Here goes*.

Quietly, slowly, she began to walk forward, and the icy dankness of the grimy passageway closed its fist around her. Her hearing became super-acute, and she was hyper-aware of the feint crunching of the ground beneath her feet, of the shallowness of her breathing, of the blood being pumped through her body. The small circle of light from her head torch illuminated the little breaths coming from her mouth. She kept the beam fixed straight ahead, waiting for an engine to appear. A silent engine, with no steam, no driver. A devil-engine.

Something caught her eye. Or rather, it was the absence of something. There was a hole in the tunnel wall to her right. It was small and round and was set into the slimy brickwork at around waist-height. Fearful of what might appear in the tunnel before her if she took her attention away for even just a second, she inched her way over to it, quickly bent down and peered in. Her head torch flickered again so she hit it. The thin beam illuminated what could only be described as a long, straight tube with no end in sight.

Don't get distracted, she told herself. *Just keep going*.

She returned to the tracks and continued to follow them, leaving the hole in the wall behind. Again, her head torch flickered.

"Fuck!" she rasped.

She stood bolt upright, rigid. Her eyes flicked back and forth. A grave silence returned to the tunnel once the echoes of her scream had died away.

Oh my days, she thought. *Just get me the hell out of here.* Her fear was taking a back seat to anger. *Why didn't I just go out on my date? Fucking Rich and his...*

But the decision to call off the date had been hers and hers alone. The only person she could get angry with was herself.

From now on, just hang out with your friends, write your stories, go to work...

Go to work! Her heart raced at the mere thought of it, and then her head torch flickered and died and Syeeda was left standing alone in an icy-cold, deathly black tunnel deep underground.

Not now! Not now!

She hit it again but she knew this was it. No more light. Now she was truly lost and alone.

Now what the fuck am I...? Hang on a minute!

She pulled her phone from her back pocket, turned it on, swiped down for a menu of commands and poised her finger over the torch setting.

Screw you, Roz, she thought, *don't ever tell me that smartphones are evil ever again*!

She activated the torch and saw that the silent engine was standing motionless on the track about two metres in front of her.

This time, the onslaught of panic did not completely blind her. As she turned to run, she had the presence of mind to hang on tightly to her mobile. It was now her only source of light, the one thing that stood between her and an unimaginable death.

I would literally die without my phone.

She risked a glance behind, flashing the beam of light. It glinted off the huge iron boiler plate riveted to the front of the monstrous vehicle. It was following her. Keeping pace with her.

"NO!" she screamed. "NO!"

Something caught her eye. Or rather, it was the absence of something. It was the hole in the wall. Only this time, as she fled from the thing that was pursuing her, it was on her left. It was a somewhere that the engine could not follow, and so she dived into it and began to crawl.

She moved through the narrow space as speedily as she could. She felt the roof of the stony tube scraping the top of her head. Beneath her hands the surface was wet and slimy. She aimed the beam of light from her phone straight ahead and saw that tube appeared to be squirming. She squinted and tried to make sense of it, and then her stomach lurched with the realisation. Spiders. The tube was crawling with spiders. Her ultimate fear. But death was following closely behind her and she had no choice but to press on. She shut her eyes, closed her mouth tightly, and crawled. Crawled fast. She could feel the spiders crunching beneath her elbows and silently she began to pray for the end of this utter nightmare.

After about half-a-minute she risked a peek ahead and saw what looked like a grille. The end of the tube! She stopped at the grille and listened. All was silent. Had she managed to evade it, whatever it was? Had it seen her darting into here? Had it just carried on along the tracks?

Her hand, the one clutching the phone, was shaking terribly. Slowly, gingerly, she pointed it back down the tube. Something black and spindly was moving toward her at inhuman speed. She screamed and scrambled desperately on in a dense fog of terror and desperation.

This was real. This was happening.

She reached the grille and shook it violently.

"COME ON!" she roared! "COME O-O-O-ON!"

The grille, weakened from decades of oxidisation, gave way and clattered down onto the floor below. She hauled herself through the hole and tumbled to the grimy ground, landing in a few inches of rancid water. She leapt to her feet, knowing that she had mere seconds to save herself before that thing, that creature, came crawling through the hole. She flashed the beam of light all around her. She was at the bottom of what appeared to be a well. Before her, opposite to the hole she had just emerged from, was a round metal door about the same height off the ground. She was trapped. She wanted to look again down the passageway – surely she had been seeing things, a trick of the light and of her terrified mind – but she could not bring herself to.

The key! She still had the key in her pocket. The one that had let them into this accursed hellhole in the first place. Shaking and fumbling, she pulled it from her pocket and tried to insert it into the keyhole. *Oh, please god, please god!* It took and she turned it. She heard a heavy locking mechanism release. She pushed the door open and threw her battered body through the hole and fell hard against the floor on the other side. With every joint painfully protesting, she shot to her feet and grabbed the round door. As she quickly pushed it shut, she caught a glimpse of two long, dark, spider-like limbs unfolding through the hole in the opposite wall. There was something inhuman down here with her. Madness tried to overtake her, but she would not let it.

"WHAT THE FUCK? WHAT THE ACTUAL LIVING FUCK?" she shouted.

With sharp, shallow breaths, she quickly took in her surroundings. She was in a long, dank passageway, but at least she could stand up. Her heart thumped against her chest, but she was not panicking. She was thinking. And what's more, she couldn't believe that she was thinking. The presence of mind that she was managing to retain in this nightmarish scenario shocked even her. And then it occurred to her why: improbably, it was because of her computer game habit. She had spent half her life playing first-person shooters like Doom, Titanfall, Call of Duty and Destiny and now she had found herself in a real-life first-person shooter scenario and her mind was already programmed to deal with it. The only difference was that she wasn't armed. And that she might actually really die. But still, her mind was solely focussed on survival. She was looking forward three or four moves. She was going to make it out of here, no matter what.

The CLANG of something striking the metal door behind jolted her back into the moment and she took off down the passageway.

If there's another way out along here, she thought, *back into the train tunnel, I should be able to double-back to where I started.*

CLANG.

Then I need to turn left so that I'll be heading away from the silent train.

The glint of light on metal up ahead caught her eye. *Another door. This one normal height. Oh god.* Had she pocketed the key after the last time? She felt for it. It was in her pocket. Again, she couldn't believe how in control she was, even when she thought her senses were leaving her.

CLANG.

The key fit the lock. She turned it and pushed. The heavy steel door did not give easily. Then she was pushing it shut behind her. Locking it. Pocketing the key. Safe.

Silence.

Nervously, she shone her light around this new space that she had found herself in. It was a room. A large round, cavernous room. Every inch of wall space was lined with books. It was a library. The library that the old man had told Rich about. But, of course, Syeeda knew nothing of this.

She noticed the floor. It was tiled in that intricate, Victorian fashion. The kind of original feature that added a small fortune onto the price of a house. And in the centre of the room stood a long table. Syeeda couldn't help noticing that it was coffin-shaped. There were eight chairs at the table, one of which was lying on its back on the floor. Next to it was another pile of dust or webs.

And on the far side, another door.

Treading lightly, she made her way slowly across this mysterious place, this secret library in the heart of a forgotten subterranean labyrinth. A cocoon at the centre of a web. Something made her stop. There was a little thought nagging at her, one which she couldn't ignore. She crept over to the edge of the room and brushed the dust off one of the book spines. Malleus Maleficarum: The Hammer of the Witches.

So it was witchcraft then. That was all she wanted to know.

Roz will want to see this, she thought, and slipped it into her coat pocket before cautiously moving on. She came to the door and took the key from her pocket. Then she paused and looked back. She aimed her beam at the heap of grey matter on the floor next to the upended chair. Despite knowing exactly what lay under it, she could not help herself. There was a compulsion too strong to ignore. She had to see it with her own eyes.

She walked over to it and steeled herself. Holding her phone with its precious beam in her right hand, she crouched down, pulled the sleeve of her coat over her left hand and very gently began to brush. The soft matter gave away easily, like old cobwebs in an abandoned house in the woods. It powdered and crumbled and dissolved into nothingness, leaving soft clouds of light dust in the air. Then she felt something hard underneath all the soft material. *This is it*, she thought. *Get ready*. She brushed and brushed and something grey-coloured began to emerge through the greyness. *Bone?* Sensing that her fear was receding, she brushed a little more vigorously. It was definitely bone. The back of a skull. Face down. A few moments later she uncovered a skeletal hand. *Someone died here trying to crawl away*, she thought.

And then she noticed that she had only 9% battery life left and felt a pang of terror.

She probably had another twelve or fifteen minutes to find her way out. Or find Roz and Fee. Where were they? Where was she, for that matter? She exited through the door and stepped into the darkness where the tunnel dweller was waiting for her.

***

The building was very inconspicuous. If she hadn't been looking for it, she never would have noticed it. But there, showing faintly through the tinted glass, was the logo for Beacon Radio.

She took out her phone and looked at the time. She was ten minutes early. The optimum time to arrive for a job interview, she thought. With what felt like the Riverdance being performed in her stomach, she hopped up the few steps and pressed the buzzer on the wall.

"Hello. Can I help?" asked a crackly voice.

"Hi. I'm here for a job interview. My name's Syeeda Khan."

The receptionist introduced herself as Karlie. She was a petite, pretty, dark-haired lady. Syeeda looked down on her from her height advantage of about a foot. Karlie led her along a muted corridor, past various offices and a row of small studios that she referred to as "bubbles". She opened a door to an empty conference room and invited Syeeda to take a seat. On the table before her was a jug of water, a glass, a sheet of A4 paper with something printed on it, a virgin notepad and a pen.

"Okay, so the interview's going to be in two parts," Karlie explained. "Firstly, there's a brief on the table there. We want you to sit here and write a commercial based on that brief. You have about twenty minutes. And then, in the second half of the interview, you'll be expected to present what you've written."

"Okay," said Syeeda.

The prospect of this did not panic Syeeda one bit. She had been doing her homework. She had been tuning in to this station pretty much non-stop since she had been called in for the interview, and for the first time in her life she had been listening – *really* listening – to the adverts. She had sussed out that there was a certain language to them, and a rhythm. Languages she was good at. Languages she could do. After all, she could already speak three: English (courtesy of her country), Punjabi (courtesy of her parents) and German (courtesy of an app). She was equipped for this. She was prepared.

"Would you like a tea or coffee while you get to work?"

"Um. No thank you. Water's fine."

"Alright. You crack on and I'll come back and get you in about twenty minutes." The receptionist put a hand on Syeeda's arm. "Good luck," she said with a little smile.

Now alone, Syeeda took a seat and read through the brief:

Client: Road Safety London
Who are we talking to: Car drivers
W h a t   d o   w e   w a n t   t h e m   t o   d o: v i s i t roadsafetylondon.org.uk
Why should they do it: The client wants a 40-second radio advertisement warning of the dangers of using a mobile phone whilst driving. Drivers are three times more likely to be involved in a road traffic accident if they are using a phone. The client would like a creative advertisement that hammers home the personal cost of not paying due care and attention when behind the wheel.

Syeeda sat back and thought for a moment. The obvious course here was to just have a stern voice telling you that using your mobile whilst driving was illegal and that blah blah blah. But what they wanted from her was creativity.

Should the script focus on the car driver at fault? Maybe not. Syeeda had a method when writing her short stories. When she came up with an idea for a tale, she would first decide from whose perspective it should obviously be told, and then she would try to write it from a different one. So if there was a good guy, she would write it from the point of view of the bad guy. If the story was about a millionaire property developer, she would approach it from the perspective of his cleaner. That sort of thing. This was her way of shaking things up, creatively speaking.

The door burst open and a tall, thin man in aviator shades and an Elvis costume took a step in. Tucked under his arm was a large, cuddly elf.

"Sorry," he said, looking as surprised as she was, and then left.

Oh yeah, thought Syeeda. *This seems like my kinda place.*

Seventeen minutes and forty-six seconds later, Karlie returned to find the interviewee sitting at the table with her arms crossed and a notepad covered with scribblings on the table in front of her.

"All done?" she asked.

"Well, it took a few goes, but I think I got there in the end." Syeeda smiled.

"Glad to hear it. Come on then. It's time for part two. You ready?"

She was.

Syeeda was led through a deserted office. "This is the sales room," Karlie explained. "They're all out getting in front of clients at the mo. Or at least, they'd better be."

They stopped at a door.

"Here we are." Karlie gave a cursory knock and opened it. "Syeeda Khan."

"Ah, Syeeda. Come in. Have a seat."

The man with the Geordie accent who greeted her was

around fifty years old, wore a checked shirt and had a friendly face. "Howdya find the brief?" he asked.

"It was fine." Syeeda smiled, shaking his hand. "I think I've managed to come up with something."

"Good. Excellent. Well, my name's Alan. Alan Shearer. But not *that* Alan Shearer."

He stopped talking, obviously waiting for some sort of response from Syeeda, but she just stared at him blankly.

"Not a football fan, then?"

Syeeda shook her head.

"Okay. Not a problem. Anyway, I'm the head of creative, and this is Amber. Amber is the station director."

An astoundingly glamorous woman in her forties with long dark hair stood up from behind the desk.

"Pleased to meet you, Syeeda," Amber said as she extended a hand.

Syeeda took it and couldn't help noticing that she was wearing leather trousers. *No suits*, she thought. This helped to put her at ease a little.

"First of all, can I just say..." Alan began as he lowered himself into his chair, "...that your covering letter really stood out. No one else thought of writing an advert for themselves when they applied. It was brilliant."

Syeeda had indeed composed an advertisement for herself which she had included with her cover letter and her CV. It went:

MVO: Can you work to tight deadlines?

ME: Yes I Khan!

MVO: Can you turn up for work on time every day, despite all the horrors that the London public transport system can throw at you?

ME: Yes I Khan!

MVO: Can you take an effective brief from a client, and then present it with absolutely no fear of making a twerp of yourself, even if you have to make chicken noises or adopt an outrageously silly accent?

ME: Yes I Khan!

MVO: And can you come up with great ideas, day after day after day, at a moment's notice?

ME: You're darn right I Khan.

Syeeda Khan. Creative genius from 1994- present.

"Thank you," said Syeeda. She was genuinely stunned that no one else had thought of doing this. It had seemed so obvious to her: you're applying for a creative position, so you submit a creative application. Duh!

"So what have you got for us?" asked Amber. "We're waiting to be dazzled."

This is it, thought Syeeda. *The future course of my life now depends on the sheet of paper that I have in my hand. Well, here goes...*

"The advert opens with the sound of a phone ringing. It's picked up. We hear a man's voice. Hello? From the other end of the phone we hear a woman. Hi, it's Janine – Janine? – Yes, Janine. We haven't seen each other in years. In fact, the last time you saw me I was only eight years old. Do you remember? – Um. No. I'm sorry. Do I know you? – You should do. I was holding my mother's hand when you hit her in your car and killed her. You were talking on your mobile phone when you were driving. *Now* do you remember?"

At this point Alan and Amber both gasped. Then they looked to each other and shared a wry little smile.

Got 'em, Syeeda thought.

Exiting the building, Syeeda, now meeting the future as a friend, puffed out her chest and walked tall in the direction of the nearest tube station. *I am a writer, she thought*, her mouth skimming over the surface of the words. *I know this because I spent several weeks agonising over a comma in my latest story. Only writers do this. I am a writer.*

The phone call came a week later, when she was sitting at her desk in her DWP office, on a cold and overcast Wednesday afternoon. She felt her mobile buzzing frantically in her back pocket and her heart ever-so-slightly jumped. Her heart had done this every single time her phone had rung since the interview. She slinked off to a quiet stairwell to answer it. The number was a withheld one.

"Hello?"

"Hi. Is this Syeeda?"

Syeeda recognised the Geordie accent immediately.

"Yes, it is. Hi there." Her nerve-endings began to tingle with excitement.

"Great. How are you doing?"

"I'm very well, thank you," *Oh god oh god oh god.* "How are you?"

"Great. Thanks for asking. So, Syeeda, how would you like to come and work in radio?"

Four minutes after the call had ended, Syeeda was still jumping up and down in the stairwell. She couldn't scream out loud, not here, so instead she did it internally. *YEEEEEEEEEEES*!

That very afternoon she handed her notice in. It was the most beautifully composed notice letter that her team leader had ever received. And as she skipped out of work that evening, the same seven words just kept rolling over and over in her brain: *The rest of my life begins now*!

Chapter Five

Ffion

She awoke to the sound of desperate screaming and to the metallic taste of blood in her mouth. Through the dense, delirious fog of her concussion, she could not tell if the screams were real or echoes of a dream or a memory.

She had no idea where she was, or when. All she knew was that she was lying face down against cold, hard gravel. She moved and an acute spasm of pain pierced her right elbow, causing her to yelp.

The screaming continued.

Syeeda?

Her focus sharpened. That *was* Syeeda. She was sure of it. Then it all came crashing in. She was in a train tunnel deep underground. She recalled the silent engine and her heart vaulted. Rich! Rich ran away and she remembered him crying out, and then...

This.

Slowly and very painfully, she raised herself from the scrabbly ground and into a kneeling position. Her right foot was weak and sore. Was it sprained? She put her hands to her face which felt hot, bruised and bloody. She winced as raw nerve endings jolted at the touch of her fingertips. The inside of her head bang bang banged like a steel hammer.

And then the screaming abruptly ceased.

Syeeda? Not you. Not you. Not my best friend!

All was still black. She felt for her head torch and whipped her fingers away as they met with broken glass. She had never felt as helpless as she did at this moment; lost and afraid, like a tiny creature caught in a trap in the middle of a mountain forest in the dead of night. Where was Syeeda? Where was Rosalind? What was going on? Was this a nightmare?

She felt a pang of hope as she recalled the phone in her pocket. It had a torch function. Where was it? It wasn't where it should be. Frantically, she ran her hands over the sharp gravel and the frigid train lines, including the one that had connected with her face about twenty minutes previously.

Something made of plastic and fibreglass found its way into her grasp.

Oh, thank god!

She pressed the button on the side to activate it, found the torch function and hit "on". And then there was light. She swept the pool of illumination around her. There was the gaping mouth of the tunnel with the train lines disappearing into it. There was the platform. There were the three stairways that led upwards from the platform. There was no sign of any of her friends. Nor was there any sign of the silent engine.

She suddenly realised that she was very, very thirsty, but she had no water. She had to get out of here. She tried calling out the name of her best friend, but her mouth did not seem to want to cooperate.

"Syeeeeda!"

It came out as a long, low drawl.

"Syeeeeeda!"

The pain was excruciating. The faces of her two beloved children presented themselves at the forefront of her mind and the will to escape and survive flexed a muscle inside her, filling her, strengthening her. She grasped the top lip of the platform, steeled herself, and then heaved. She drew herself upright as spasms of white-hot pain ignited in her right foot. Definitely sprained.

The shot of pain, however, did help to clear her mind. Mentally, she was back in the room now. Focused. If I can stand then I can hobble. If I can hobble, then I can leave.

The platform was at waist-height against her. Knowing that she couldn't possibly step or hop up onto it, she instead turned her back to it, lifted her behind onto it so that she was in a sitting position, swung her feet up and then slowly, agonisingly, stood up.

She shone the light from her phone in the direction of the three stairway entrances. *The one on the right*, she remembered. She began to hobble in the direction of the furthermost of the tunnels, but then something stopped her. A prickly sense of cold dread. Understandable, really. With her hand shaking violently, she aimed the beam of light from her phone up the stairway. There was no movement, but the light caught something lying on the ground. It glinted back at her. It was something plastic or metal. Ffion had a feeling she knew what it was, and so, slowly and agonisingly, she shuffled forward.

As she had suspected, it was Rich's camera.

"Rich?" she whispered. "Rich?" She knew that he was not there, but she had to try.

With the camera in one hand and her phone in the other, giving her light, she examined the tiny black buttons on the side of it. She unfolded the viewfinder and pressed the 'on' button. The screen flickered into grey life and she saw an image appear. It was her feet.

She tried to resist rewinding the footage that Rich had already shot. She feared dreadfully that whatever horror it was that had taken her friends would appear again if she gave life to it on the small screen. But she could not help herself. She felt compelled. She had to see. To see if it was actually real, whatever it was. Real enough to be captured in microscopic pixels.

She flopped herself down onto a step and laid the phone down next to her so that it projected its thin beam onto the ceiling above. The light was a comfort. She felt safer with it. The camera trembled in her hands. She pressed her lips together and pressed 'back'. After a few seconds she stopped it and pressed 'play'.

"Rich, you're not really gonna come back here on your own, are you, like you said?" It was her own voice.

"No, I don't think so," came the quiet reply.

"Rich," Ffion whispered, and gently ran her fingers over the viewfinder. An image of his daughter Mimi's smiling face flashed across her mind.

"I'll...er...come back with other people. I don't know. Like the authorities or something, I suppose. It's going to take a professional team to map all this. And see what those things are."

Ffion held the 'forward' button down for roughly four seconds, watching the image on the screen whiz on. Then she released it and the playback resumed.

"Roz. What are we going to do?"

Again, it was her own voice. Wide-eyed, she watched as herself, Syeeda and Roz edged their way downward towards the platform. Between them came fleeting glimpses of the silent engine. Ffion's flesh rippled with icy goosebumps.

And then, there it was. The big rusting iron hulk, eerily still, filling the frame. Seeing it in this context took some of the horror out of it. It was no longer spectral. Its sheer solidity rendered it real. It was a thing, just like everything else was a thing. An object.

Rosalind stepped forward and slowly reached a hand out towards the boiler.

Ffion's stomach tightened. *This is it*, she thought.

Despite knowing full well what was coming, she still jumped when it happened. First it was the screaming. Rich's screaming. Cold, distant and tinny through the camera's tiny speaker. And then the blurring of motion. She could just about make out Rich's feet, running, with the ground flying by below.

"OH GOD NO! NOOOOOOOOOOOOOOOO!"

Ffion, her breath held, felt a wave of prickly heat wash over her.

"OH GOD PLEASE NO PLEASE NO OOOOOH MY GOD NOOOO!"

She wanted to turn the camera off and throw it away, but she couldn't. She had to know. She had to see. And then there it was, and time seemed to stop dead.

It was onscreen for less than a second; a silhouetted figure caught in time. Was it a man? It was tall and thin, but perhaps *too* tall and thin. And the way it moved? Could a person really move like that? It was so fast. It was humanoid, but at the same time there was something very inhuman about it. She had seen enough.

Ffion let the camera fall to the ground and the sound of Rich begging for his life ceased. For a few minutes she sat there in the pale light, her short, sharp breaths turning to freezing mist in front of her. She was going to die down here, and the worst thing about it was that she would not be able to say goodbye to her boys, to Geraint and Iwan. For the rest of their lives there would be that pain in their hearts, that longing, because one day their mother had been there and then the next...she had not. By never knowing why, without that explanation, they would never be able to put her to bed inside their young minds and move on. She would never become compartmentalised. They would be haunted by her for the rest of their lives.

She did not want to cause them pain. She did not want to be responsible for any lingering suffering. She had to get a message to them somehow. She had to.

Again, she picked up Rich's camera, pressed 'record' and pointed it at herself. Thankfully, the viewfinder was now pointing away from her, so she couldn't see the bloody mess of her face. For this she was grateful, but she knew that she would have to spare her sons this trauma as well.

"Gregg. It's me. It's Ffion," she began, her voice small, broken and frightened. "Before I start you have to promise me one thing. You have to promise me never to show this to my boys. They can't ever see their mother like this. They just can't. So you're going to have to tell them everything that I say in this video, okay? Promise me that."

She paused for a moment, eyes closed, and thought about how to begin.

"First of all, I am so, so sorry. I am so sorry that I ever agreed to come here today and do this. I should have stayed at home with you and Geraint and Iwan. But I did come and now I'm lost and I'm not going to make it home and you're going to have to bring up the boys for me, okay? I'm deep underground in a railway tunnel and I've got no way to get out. And there's something down here with us and I think it killed Rich and maybe Syd too and I think it's coming for me next. And I don't know where Rosalind is. Oh god, I hope she got out. I hope she got out."

Her face was hot, and her eyes were starting to burn.

"I know it's a few weeks away yet, but I started buying you birthday presents. There's a shoebox under the bed and there's a few little prezzies in there so you can have those on your birthday, okay? I hope you find them. And I took Iwan's coat to be fixed at the market. You know, the one the zip broke off. So you'll have to go and get that because winter's coming and he's going to need his coat."

And then the flood came.

"I'm so sorry, my gorgeous darling man. I'm so sorry. Just know that I love you, okay? I really truly love you. And tell the boys, tell Geraint and Iwan that their mammy loves them too. Make sure they know that their mammy loves them and misses them, and she'll be with them forever. They have to know that. They have to know. Kiss them goodnight for me every night and tell them, okay? Tell them every night. Goodbye, my beautiful man. I love you."

She knew that this place would not remain lost forever. Nothing ever did. One day, and she hoped it would be soon, people would come and they would swarm all over the place with their floodlights and their walkie-talkies and their hardhats and they would map and chart every last corner of it, and that thing – whatever that thing was – would be driven out by the light and the talk and the normality. And eventually they would find her and this camera, and connections would be made, and the message would be delivered into Gregg's hands and then passed on to her boys and then they would know that their mother had truly gone and they'd be able to grieve and move on. They'd be able to live and grow and become the people that they were meant to be, and her loss would make them stronger.

Yes. Something good would come of this. She lowered the

camera and felt a kind of calm fall over her. The calm that embraces someone when they know that the end truly has come, and that all hope is gone. She sat there in the cold, gloomy silence for a moment or two. Then, for no particular reason whatsoever she picked up her phone again, activated the torch and shone it up the stairway. A little further up from where she was sitting was a big pile of dust or cobwebs or whatever they were. She felt certain that Rich lay under there.

Poor Rich, she thought. *Poor Mimi.*

And then she noticed that lying next to it was Rich's backpack. Her curiosity peaked, and she drew herself up and hobbled up to it. She lowered herself to her knees and opened it. Carefully, methodically, she pulled the contents from it and laid them in a line on the step before her.

There was an array of batteries all tied up together in a plastic bag. Then there was a map. The map! Then some funny-looking goggles. They were heavy and bulky. Were these the night-vision goggles? The SAS ones? And then there was another map. Or was this a plan or a blueprint? Either way, it could come in very handy. And then there was a large torch. Now THAT was more like it.

Hope began gushing through her and it felt exhilarating! She was not going to die down here at the hands of that...thing after all! She had everything she needed here to get out, and that was exactly what she was going to do. No matter what! She was going to get out and go straight to the police and tell them everything so that they could come and rescue Rosalind. And Geraint and Iwan were not going to lose their mother. Not today.

Ffion took up the torch, hit the button and in the circle of light saw a dark, spindly creature with glowing eyes racing towards her at supernatural speed.

***

SYD: Hey fee! U still coming tomoz??? ☺ ☺ ☺
FEE: Yeh you?

SYD: Sure am!

FEE: Thought u had a date

SYD: Called it off. Rather come out with u guyz ☺

FEE: Nice 1syd. Glad ur comin. Wuldnt be same without u

SYD: Aw thanks fee. Luv u too! ♥♥♥

FEE: Shut up mun

SYD: So wot time we meeting tomoz

FEE: Roz sez at 7

SYD: 7??? No way!!! So much for my lie in!!!

FEE: I know. Me too. Cant believe roz is comin

SYD: Me 2. Didnt think wed eva get her down a dirty old underground

FEE: Love roz tho. Shes great

SYD: Yeh shes Fabio.

FEE: U scared?

SYD: Of wot???

FEE: Going down there. I am. Im scared of the dark me

SYD: What??? Then why u comin???

FEE: Rich said hed pay me

SYD: Rich is paying u??? How much???

FEE: 50 quid

Chapter Six

Rosalind

She had heard screaming, but it had been indistinct, distant. Screams upon screams upon screams were ricocheting around the tunnel system like atoms in a Hadron Collider. There was no possible way for her to discern which direction they were coming from. They seemed to be coming from all directions. And nor could she discern which of her friends it was. But when the terrible noise began to multiply and swirl around in the darkness it froze her to the core, and she knew that her life could never be the same again.

She was hopelessly lost in this dark, labyrinthine sub-city. When the silent engine had come, fear, panic and confusion had swept through them like wildfire and, like the others, her first instinct had been to run. She had started running with Ffion and Syeeda, but she had witnessed Ffion vanishing into nothingness. One moment she was there, the next she wasn't. And in that brief moment of distraction, Syeeda too had disappeared. She tried to replay the sequence of events in her mind's eye but all she saw and heard was noise, flashes of light and rapid movement.

And now she was alone with no idea how to get back to where this had all started. She had escaped into the tunnel mouth, following the train tracks until she saw what looked like a small service passageway off to the side. Into it she had fled, crouching down so as not to hit her head on the low ceiling.

There had been a turning to the left, so she had taken it. A turning to the right. She had taken that too. There *really was* something with them down here in the darkness, and there was only one thing occupying her mind - survival. If there was something behind her, something following her, she wanted to lose it, to throw it off the scent. The trouble is, did that also mean that she would never be able to find her way back out?

And now here she was, sitting on the floor, back against the wall, hot with sweat and cold with fear. Her body was exhausted but her mind hyperaware. A sound from somewhere in the darkness found her ear. It sounded like: "What the fuck? What the fuck?"

Rosalind shot up, standing to attention, stiff and rigid, waiting. The shouting was followed by a metallic clang. And then another clang. And then another.

"Something's happening," she whispered sharply to no one but herself. "That was Syeeda. I know that was Syeeda!"

"SYEEDA!" she screamed. She was running, trying to retrace her steps. "SYD!" She took a right turn and then a left. And then she hit a dead end. Confused she spun around several times, trying to make sense of it all. She turned to run back but her foot caught on something and she fell. She held her hands out in front of her and hit the wet ground hard. Looking back, she saw that there was a hatch on the floor. She had tripped over the handle.

She felt like a wild animal cornered. With nothing to lose and a friend possibly within finding-distance, she leapt at the hatch, turned the handle and opened it up. Aiming her head torch down the hole, she saw that there were rungs sticking out of the side. *A ladder*! Down she went.

She jumped the last few rungs and landed up to her ankles in rancid water. The water was alive. It squirmed and wriggled and thrashed around her feet. She tried to make sense of it, and then she realised. Rats! Hundreds of them. They began biting at her feet, but she was protected by her DM's. She screamed, kicked and ran. The rats cleared out of her way as she rampaged past. Some followed, squealing and biting.

Rosalind emerged into yet another passageway of darkness absolute. It was wide and the ceiling was high. It seemed to curve around a central structure. "SYEEDA!" she called again. Nothing. She picked a direction and ran, leaving the remaining rats behind.

Eventually, up ahead, she saw an end to the corridor. It was opening up into a larger space. Her heart began to beat faster and faster as she neared. And then she found herself standing in a large lightless room. She methodically swept it with her head torch, surveying it thoroughly. To her right was a big, metal door. It looked like it weighed several tonnes. Her pool of light swept onto the floor, illuminating a pile of grey dust and cobwebs, causing a sharp intake of breath. She put her hand to her mouth and stared wide-eyed. Somehow she knew, just knew, that this was all that was left of Syeeda.

Her mind raced, searching for a way to undo this. To turn the clock back and renege on all the decisions that had led her and her dear friends to this dreadful place, to this awful moment and to this grisly fate. But there was no way. What had been done could not be undone. Syd was dead.

Her stomach twisted and lurched and her pores oozed hot sweat over clammy skin. Sick with fear and heartache, she vomited. The process was painful and acidic and left her feeling drained. She dropped to her knees and prayed for an end to this horrible, claustrophobic nightmare.

She longed to give her friend one last hug, one last kiss, but nothing remained of her. It was as if she had died centuries ago and time had claimed her flesh and bones, leaving only dust.

"Oh, Syeeda," she moaned. "My poor, dear Syeeda. I'm so sorry. I'm so very, very sorry. Oh, please. Oh, please. I'm so, so sorry."

But as sad and broken and spent as she was, a part of her knew that she still had to get out of here. She had to get back to Phil. She had to get back to her boys. She felt a sharp stab of guilt as she thought of them, Callum and Nathan. She had sent them out into the world to make them stand on their own feet, to become men, but they were still only children. What had she done? She longed to hold them close. To hug them and kiss them and tell them how much she loved them. She had to get back to them. Back to them all. Back to her family.

She had to live, no matter what.

"Goodbye, my beautiful friend," she whispered through hot tears to all that remained of her friend. "I love you. I'm sorry." She blew her a kiss.

As she was about to stand, she noticed something lying on the ground nearby. It looked like a book. She picked it up and aimed her head torch at the cover. Malleus Maleficarum: The Hammer of Witchcraft. The title alone chilled her. Was this book somehow connected to what had happened here? To the situation they had found themselves in. Had Syeeda retrieved this from somewhere, and if so where? And had she retrieved it for her?

All these thoughts flashed through her mind. But her first priority was to leave, to live. The outside pockets on her coat were large enough to accommodate the book, and so she slipped it into one of them. She looked around the large sparse room that she had found herself in. Something glinted in the torchlight, something golden or brass. It was the key. Rosalind scooped it up and pocketed that too.

She refocused her mind on getting out of here. There was the huge, metal door that she had already seen, and facing that, in the opposite wall, was a round grille about three feet in diameter. She peered through the bars and saw that it covered a tube that stretched away for about twenty feet. There was another grille at the far end. She clocked that the tube was big enough for her to crawl through, if need be. She marched up to the door and tried pushing it and then pulling it. It was locked solid. No use. So her options were to carry on following the passageway around the central structure – but she was pretty sure that that would just lead her back to her present situation – to try and climb back up the manhole she just dropped out from – not really an option at all as she would just go back to being lost – or to try and heave the grille out of the wall, crawl through and see where that led to.

As much as she really didn't want to crawl through a tight hole in the deep, cold darkness with some unknown entity potentially scouring the labyrinth for her, right now it felt like her best option. She wrapped her fingers around the bars, braced one foot against the wall and heaved with all her remaining strength. The grille gave way without any resistance and she fell backwards onto the floor, the grille landing on top of her.

"FUUUUUCK!" she screamed. She shot to her feet and threw the grille against the great iron door. The noise it made upon collision was horrific, and so was the noise it made when it crashed onto the floor. It was a like a metallic scream that went slicing through her head and away through the tunnels and passages, circling back around several times before finally dying out.

"Oh, fuck," Rosalind whispered. "Perhaps I shouldn't have done that." She knew that that sound would have echoed through every single part of this abysmal sub-city, alerting whoever it was, whatever it was, to her presence. She had to move fast.

She pushed herself into the tube and began to crawl. The surface was cold and slimy and the book in her pocket dug into her, but she kept on moving, shuffling along on her elbows. She heard a scratching sound above her. She craned her neck and saw that the roof of the tube was crawling with black spiderswith shiny backs and armoured legs, just like beetles. She swallowed a scream and shuffled on as quickly as she could, keeping her head down, biting her lip. Spiders dropped onto her head and into her path. She crunched on through them regardless until she reached the grille at the far end. Peeking out through the bars, she could see train tracks on the ground. She was back in a train tunnel, exactly where she didn't want to be. But she knew that time to pontificate about this fact was a luxury that she did not have, so she pushed against the grille, hoping that it would give way as easily as the first one. It did, and it clanged onto the ground below, creating another monstrous, tinny cacophony.

She squeezed out of the hole and onto the gravelly ground. She had completely lost her bearings and had absolutely no idea whether she should run to the left or to the right. She wanted to get back to the station that she and her friends had originally emerged onto, where they had seen the silent engine, where Ffion had vanished, where Rich had...had...

If she could make it back there and take the stairway on the right and turn left at the top, she was pretty sure she could find her way back out, and so she picked a direction and started running, following the train tracks. Up head, all she could see was the tunnel arch curving away and around to the right. Beyond that, just shadow. Her senses were incredibly heightened with the grim expectation of something emerging from the unknowing gloom at any moment. She glanced behind, casting the small pool of light generated by her head torch. Again, there was only the curve of the tunnel and shadow.

She ran on. *I can do this,* she told herself. *I can do this. I can get out and get help. I can do this. I can do this. Just keep moving forward. Just keep moving forward.*

She risked another glance behind. The only thing following her was the darkness. "Come on, come on, come on. You can do this. Keep moving forward. Keep moving forward."

She looked back again and the silent engine was rolling along the tracks immediately behind her. An avalanche of panic and horror engulfed her, and she screamed and sprinted away.

"OH NO, NO, NO, NO, NO, NO!"

She looked back and saw that the engine was keeping pace with her.

"H E E E E E E E E E E E E E L P ! " s h e s c r e a m e d. "HEEEEEEEEEEEEELP!" But all her friends were already dead.

Ahead, Rosalind saw the tunnel open out into a cavern. Was this a station? There was a platform and three stairways, so yes it was. Was it *the* station? She had no way of knowing. She went to leap up onto the platform, but her foot caught on the track and she crashed head first into the wall.

She came to just a few seconds later. Opening her eyes, she saw her own hands and the ground, but all was flickering. Was it her vision? No, it was her head torch. She had smashed it when she had fallen. Woozy and bloody, she got onto her hands and knees and in the intermittent light saw the silent engine approaching. It was about to run over her.

"Oh god! Oh god!" she panted. She hauled herself to her feet and rolled onto the platform as the engine passed noiselessly and steamlessly by. And then it stopped. She got up and ran, heading for the stairway on the right. She entered and began to sprint upwards, and then, in the pulsating light, something overcame her.

Rosalind realised that she could barely move. She felt as if she was sinking into the ground. She gasped and pushed and tried to move her body forward, but every limb felt like it had been turned to clay. She began to grow desperate and her breathing became rapid and shallow. *I don't want to die*, a voice inside her head screamed. *I don't want to die!*

Her vision began to turn grey, as if her eyes were being clouded by billowing sheets of ancient, dusty cobwebs. Her body grew heavier and heavier. She was being dragged downwards, down to the grimy floor with the spiders and the rats.

Is this how it ends? she thought.

Somewhere deep inside her, she uncovered a reserve of strength and she began to fight it, fight it as angrily as she could. She found that once again she could move her arms. She pawed at her face to clear her eyes. She then realised that she had been completely enveloped by the cobwebs. They were heavy, weighing down upon her like a great, grey mountain. She grasped and pawed and pulled and the cobwebs fell away, and she scrambled back to her feet to run away.

She realised then that this was what had happened to her friends. This was the nightmare that they had been forced to endure before finding peace. This was how they had died, and now it was her turn.

Again, she began to grow heavy and to sink down. *It's feeding on me*, she thought. *It's feeding on...*

Death beckoned as the greyness engulfed her. Cold, grey desolation. Surrendering to it seemed so easy. *Just give up fighting and let it take me. Sleep. Just sleep.* But she was not ready to go. She loved her life. She loved Phil and Callum and Nathan and her house and her job and her life and she was not willing to die.

"YOU WILL NOT TAKE ME!" she roared, and the tunnel dweller lost its grip on her. She clawed at her face, pulling the cobwebs and the dust away once again.

"YOU WILL NOT TAKE ME!" She felt its power over her drainingas the blood and strength returned to her eyes and her mind and her muscles.

"YOU WILL NOT TAKE ME, YOU BASTARD!" In her anger, she had again found strength. She scrambled to her feet and ran, and then she saw two piles of grey dust and webs on the damp steps, as if huddled together. Ffion and Rich. Both gone. And once again everything drained from her, but this time it was not the creature's doing.

She slumped down onto the ground, her back up against the slimy wall. Her friends were all gone now. What was the point? There was no way out. It was over. Best to just give up and let it take her. Her head torch continued to flicker, and in the intermittent light she saw something further back down the tunnel. It appeared to be a man.

He was simply standing there, looking at her. Details were hard to discern, but he seemed to be wearing a uniform. Rosalind could definitely make out a heavy, navy-coloured coat with brass buttons, and a peaked cap. A train driver's uniform? He was standing limply, as if struggling to hold his frame upright. Then he started staggering forward, and that's when Rosalind noticed that the flesh on his face was putrefied.

At this moment, somewhat miraculously, Rosalind felt a knot of pity swelling in her breast. *Who are you?* She thought. *What happened to you?* And then: *Who did this to you?*

As he drew near, the man began to transform. His limbs and his fingers elongated, and the clothes faded away. He ceased to be a man and became a thing. An it. A creature. He was the engine driver. He was the tunnel dweller.

As it reached its full height of over seven foot, it occurred to Rosalind that gravity did not apply to it. Its movements were no longer like those of a person, and it was not subject to the physical laws of existence as were other living creatures. Its white eyes glowed faintly, as if something was burning behind them, and it reeked of age and dust and decay.

The creature was now more arachnid than humanoid. Surrendering movement on two legs for four, it crawled onto the wall and up around the ceiling, moving slowly, deliberately, and with purpose and intelligence. It bared down on Rosalind from above, positioning its arms and legs around the stricken woman, trapping her as if in a cage. All Rosalind could do was stare dumbly. She noticed that its long, brown limbs were coated with thin hairs.

Rosalind continued to breathe in short shallow gasps. She was cold and clammy with sweat now and she was shivering.She contemplated this demon that had wrapped itself around her, trapping her. Predator and prey. She was his now. It was all over, and a strange sensation of relief overcame her. It was as if a switch had been flicked. She felt somehow removed from thissituation, as if she were witnessing it all unfold on a cinema screen. Was this her mind's way of dealing with the trauma? *How strange*, she thought.

She held her breath as the tunnel dweller's fingers gripped her shoulders, and twitched as icy electrical barbs flashed through her nerve endings. It occurred to Rosalind then that this was the most horrible thing about this creature: its hands. Its hands and its fingers were thin, spindly and grasping. And then it moved its head in close, so that they were eye to glowing eye.

Rosalind's eyes darted back and forth and up and down, taking in every detail. The creature, that a few moments ago had appeared as a man, no longer seemed to be made of flesh. Its bones were bound taught by something else, and it disgusted her. She remembered something a friend of her had once said. A theory as to why so many people had such a visceral, gut-wrenching fear of house spiders: because they look like they were born inside out. They looked like an arrangement of bone and sinew that could somehow live and hunt and kill without the need for flesh.

And then there was Phil, flashing through her mind's eye. And there were her boys, Nathan and Callum. And her friends, Fee and Syd and Rich. And there was Jason who had noisily handed her a bacon butty this morning. And there were all the people she worked with whose company she loved and enjoyed. And then came all the faded faces from her tribe. The rude boys and girls. These were the ones who had helped to raise her and shape her and become the person that she was always meant to be. And here at last were her parents. But only just, for she had only known them for a few short years. So sad.

And her biggest regret? Strangely, never having the opportunity to personally thank Pauline Black from The Selector for saving her. For igniting the fire inside that young brown girl, newly arrived from Sierra Leone, all those years ago. For teaching her, through music, that hiding away was not an option. That life was most definitely worth living.

Ironic, really.

As she considered all this, Rosalind felt her gut heave, but she kept it down. The tunnel dweller, still eye to eye with her, opened its maw and presented two rows of silver, needle-sharp teeth, dripping with saliva, its breath stinking of rotten meat. *This is it*, Rosalind thought, *this is the end*. And as she narrowed her eyes and prepared to die, two words casually presented themselves at the forefront of her mind - Monster Munch.

* * *

Rosalind ran a hand through her short, greying hair. She had always worn it short. It was part of the rude girl look.

Back in 2007, a lifetime ago, it seemed, she had taken her not unwilling sons to see an exhibition of youth fashion, photography and memorabilia at the V&A. Hand in hand in hand, they had followed the trail through the late seventies and into the early eighties. Quietly and politely, her boys had listened as their mum reeled off stories and memories and reminiscences brought back to life by the exhibits.

She brought them to a stop in front of a monochrome photograph displayed on an oversized canvas. On it were three teenage girls, all DM boots and cut-off t-shirts and attitude, frozen together forever in one immaculate moment.

"What do you think of this one?" she asked.

"I like the girl who's smiling," answered Nathan.

Rosalind considered the girl in the photograph, the only one not trying just a little bit too hard to project an image of threat. The only one who looked relaxed and happy in her own skin. Neither Nathan nor Callum realised that they were actually looking at their own mother as a teenager.

Rosalind had bought a copy of the exhibition book, a small token of immortality, which was now sitting high on a shelf in her Acton home. The home she would soon be vacating.

"You know, it's not going to feel like home until this baby is hung up on the wall," said Phil. Rosalind looked over. He was holding in his hands his most prized possession, a framed LP. It was Black Sabbath's debut album, a first pressing, of course, released in 1970. Beneath the glass, the gatefold cover was open, revealing the inverted cross which contained the track listing and a poem. Also, and this is what, in the eyes of its owner, made it almost as precious as his own children, if not more so: it had been autographed by Ozzy, Tony, Geezer and Bill. The original members. The Sab Four.

"It'll feel like a home," said Rosalind, "when I've got my feet up on the sofa with a glass of wine in my hand." At that particular moment, she had her feet up on the sofa with a glass of wine in her hand.

"I can't bring myself to box this up," he said, still gazing longingly at his signed album. "You know. As we're only moving up the road, are we even going to bother with boxes?"

"Of course we are," said Rosalind. "What else are we

going to carry stuff in? Tesco bags? We're just not going to bother with a van."

"Yeah, but either way we'll have to have a bloody severe clear-out first."

"Mm. I'm actually looking forward to it. I love a purge. It's a right royal pain in the arse at the time but it always feels pretty satisfying after the fact."

"It does. It's like detoxing."

"I suppose it is. Kind of." As she said this, Rosalind's phone went ping. She reached over to the small table at her side and picked it up.

"Is that Rich again?"

"No. Syeeda this time. She's asking if I'm still going tomorrow."

"I'm assuming you are."

"Correct. Hang on. Let me just text her back." Rosalind placed her glass down and slowly typed a reply, one letter at a time, using the forefinger of her right hand. She had never mastered the art of texting with thumbs.

"So what time are you off?"

"Meeting at Jason's cafe at seven."

"And what time are you home?"

"God knows. We're venturing into unknown territory here." Rosalind narrowed her eyes. "You're asking a lot of questions."

"Just want to be able to plan my day around you, that's all."

That's all, my backside, Rosalind thought. *I can read you like a book, mate. You're up to something.*

And she was right. Phil *was* up to something. As soon as Rosalind was safely underground, he would be zooming off to Reading to pick up his mother. Then he'd be coming back into London and collecting their two boys from Victoria Coach Station before bringing them all home. Then Mika, Rosalind's friend since childhood, would be joining them. And all this would be done, hopefully, by the time Rosalind walked in.

The gathered gang would all shout "SURPRISE!", and

that would be Phil's cue to call their favourite Chinese and order in an eye-wateringly enormous takeaway. It was a little goodbye party for the house that they had lived in for the entire duration of their married life, and the house that Nathan and Callum had grown up in.

"So what are you up to?" Rosalind asked.

"Oh. Nothing."

Rosalind let it go. She was tired and she did not have the energy to perform an interrogation. And besides, she trusted Phil and Phil trusted her. She knew that whatever he was up to, it was not going to be anything bad. It never was. Rosalind reached for her Kindle as Phil considered his impressive vinyl collection.

"I hope you're going to put something relaxing on," said Rosalind.

Phil slipped a Motorhead LP from the wall of records and headed for the stereo.

"I said something relaxing," she added, eyebrow arched. Phil muttered something under his breath and returned to the shelves.

"This relaxing enough for you?" It was Alice Cooper Goes to Hell.

Rosalind gave him one of her extra-special looks. It said, *Don't even think about it*.

"Look, I'm suffering a severe emotional trauma here," she said. "You know who I always turn to when I need moral support."

Phil regarded his wife, stretched out on the sofa, wine in hand, Mr Darcy sleeping serenely next to her.

"I have to say," he ventured. "You don't look like you're suffering a severe emotional trauma."

"Don't be fooled. Moving house is one of the most stressful things you can do in life. My general demeanour may belie an appearance of serenity and control, but inside I'm a raging tsunami of hatred and fury, so you know what you have to do."

"Sounds like I've been telt," Phil said with a sigh.

"You have. Well and truly."

Rosalind was a rude girl, into 2-tone, and Phil was a rocker. Between them, they made one perfectly formed rude-rocker. Their marriage had been a blast, with no regrets to speak of from either side. They shared everything, including the hope that this would be their last ever house move.

Phil ran a finger along through the wall of vinyls, pulled out Too Much Pressure by The Selector and placed it reverentially on the turntable. As the drum intro of Three Minute Hero leapt from the speakers, he wandered over to the window and gazed out.

"I just had a thought. We're not going to be able to see the mural from our new house."

"Evidently we did not think this through," replied Rosalind with a hint of sarcasm.

Across the road and a few doors up there was a house with a mural on the side. The mural, crudely done, depicted a naked man hanging from a window. Legend had it that had been done years previously by a member of Mott the Hoople. It was a little piece of rock history in their very own street.

"I guess I'll just have to wander down the street now and then to look at it," said Phil, deploying the sarcasm-launcher himself. He stood there quietly for a moment, wondering how to frame his next question. "So, tomorrow then?"

"Mm?"

"Don't take this the wrong way, but what's the point?"

"What's the point?"

"What's the endgame? I know Rich reckons he knows where a hidden Victorian underground is and everything, but what's the actual purpose of tomorrow's exercise? Is it just to film it and prove it, or...?"

"Basically, it's so he can get divorced," Rosalind stated flatly, looking up from her Kindle.

"Exsqueeze me?"

"Yep. 'Fraid so. Rich wants out of his marriage."

"Oh, yes?"

"Yeah. So traditionally, when someone wants out of a marriage and they don't have the courage to tell their other half – they can't face having THAT conversation – they act more and more intolerably until finally it's the partner who says, 'I've had enough, I'm off', and then THEY leave. So it's all THEIR fault. And the person who originally wanted the divorce gets to be the aggrieved party and it's the partner who's the bad guy.

"However, hats off to Rich, it seems he's found a route even more convoluted than that. His big plan is to make shit loads of money so he can use it to cushion the blow."

"I see."

"Yeah. So he can give Marie a great big wedge of cash and then say, 'I'm off'. And then he can live comfortably knowing that he hasn't just abandoned his wife and child to a life of penury and destitution."

"So how's finding a Victorian underground going to get him rich?"

"He's planning on monetising the discovery by filming it all and posting it on social media. He's done the math as they say across the pond, and apparently it's viable."

"So what does he need you guys for?"

"He said that he wants me, Syd and Fee to be the friendly faces of the video. He wants to make it 'accessible', he says. In order to make money, it has to have wider appeal than to just the urban explorer crowd, or to historians. He reckons that the average punter will experience the joy and excitement of discovering these long-lost mysterious tunnels through us. It just makes it more entertaining I suppose."

"Interesting."

"Yep. He hasn't said as much, but he's cast us like actors."

"Like actors? How do you mean?"

"I'm the brains, Syd's the beauty..." Rosalind paused.

"And Fee?"

"Fee's the comic relief. Or at least, that's how I reckon he sees her, anyway."

"So why *are* you going?"

"I like Rich. He's interesting. He may be a bit of a plonker sometimes, but when he gets his teeth into a project he's like some mad professor. He just can't let it go. I admire that in a person. And, if he really is going to uncover some great Victorian mystery, I want in."

"Yeah. Figures."

"And besides, I get to spend the day with Fee and Syd. It'll be fun."

"Well, I have to say, it all sounds pretty scary to me."

"Well, you know how it is, darling. When you get to our age it's anything for a bit of adventure, isn't it?"

Chapter Seven

The mind is a curious thing. It remembers everything yet can recall very little. And what it cannot recall it reconstructs, as if reconstructing a memory is an easier task than recalling one. As I say, curious.

I experienced much during my short life and was fortunate enough, when the end came, to die in possession of a head full of memories; some of them wonderful, many of them not.

With the illumination of hindsight, they all seem to irrevocably lead to one inevitable conclusion. As if that conclusion, in other words, the moment of my death, had been preordained. Sometimes I wonder if there had been a divine hand at work, ushering and nudging me towards my grotesque fate.

Curiously, however, despite everything, I am still in a position to share some of my memories with you, and I will do so now in the hope that you may understand a little more fully.

This first one is most certainly a recollection (as opposed to a reconstruction), and a very vivid one at that:

I am a fireman. It is my job to keep the fire in the boiler of the 7800 Manor Class burning so that it may continue to thunder along the tracks until it reaches its destination. It is hard work, physical work, but I love it. We are snaking our noisy way through the still magnificence of the north Wales landscape. We have been on a steady incline for miles now, and keeping this iron monster moving forward requires backbreaking toil, and I am shovelling coal for all that I am worth. Curiously, it is the muscles in the backs of my young arms, as opposed to any others, that are suffering the most. I know not why.

We left the city many hours ago. It was a relief to bid goodbye to the grime and the bricks and the sooty air. I longed to breathe the breath of the mountains and the valleys. I find it cleansing. I observed with wonder the transformation in the scenery conjured by the mileage. Slowly, the stones became rocks, the hills became bare, the walls became dry, the grass grew long and wild and the tips of the mountains disappeared into wreaths of grey cloud.

The city, with its tides of folk washing relentlessly back and forth according to the whims of factory whistles, now felt like a memory all of its own.

Our mission is to bring Snowdonian slate to the world. It is grey gold, and there is nothing I would rather have over my head when I fall asleep at night. It is the same for both paupers and kings.

The wild and windswept countryside gives way to a scene of utter desolation, but one that possesses a strange beauty all of its own. We are now passing through the smoking industrial slag heaps of Blaenau Festiniog, and this is where we begin our ascent towards the great mountain range.

The combined cacophony of our engine, steam and whistle cracks the eerie silence of the villages as we trundle through. These are not like the village that I grew up in; tranquil, idyllic, with thatched cottages built of solid, reliable stone and nestled in lush, green countryside, abundant with vegetables and fish. No, these are mountain villages, hewn from slate. The cottages look more carved than built, as if they were chiselled into shape from the side of the mountain itself. There is not a soul to be seen, for everyone who resides here toils in the mines by day. It is a ghostly and colourless scene.

Our destination is close now but still out of sight, for a great phantom of raincloud has enveloped it utterly. The driver jerks a thumb towards the boiler. Taking the hint, I pick up my shovel. My arms ache at the mere thought of more labour. Then he sounds the whistle and we slip into the cold, damp nothingness.

The rocks, the boulders, the grass, the sheep, the mountains and the sky cease to exist. The whole world has vanished, and I am gripped by horror. I feel as if I am being cocooned, that the world is closing in on me, suffocating me. This despite the fact that all around me is a void, an absence, an emptiness. The greyness begins to devour me. I am fading away. I claw at my eyes to try and tear away the mist, but mist is intangible. I might as well try grasping at ghosts. My hands flail through the fog, gaining no purchase, no relief from the nightmare.

Control. Control is slipping away from me. My breathing grows quick and shallow, my heart thunders, sending blood surging through my young veins.

I remember shouting at first. Shouting for help. Then screaming. And finally, just panting. Something grabbed hold of my wrists. Was it the driver or...or...

The following is neither a recollection nor a reconstruction of a memory. Instead, it is a recollection of a reverie. Of a thing that might have come to pass but ultimately did not:

To choose a life on the footplate is to accept a second skin, one consisting of engine oil, grease, soot and sweat. One forgets how it feels to be clean and fresh and sweet-smelling. But now, as I traverse a busy Beak Street, that is exactly how I feel. In addition, I am glowing, as if I have a boiler smouldering warmly inside me, just like the engines that I drive. And it is just as well, because this day is a very cold one indeed. Evening has just begun to slip into night and snow is falling. The sweet sound of a choir manages to weave its way through the din of horses' hooves clip-clopping on cobbles and gently kiss my ear. It is a childrens' choir, and it is a heavenly sound.

People hurry past without so much as looking up. All are wrapped up warm against the freezing air, and everyone appears grimy and soot covered. Everyone but myself, that is. I stare with fascination as my fellow Londoners stream by;

their faces glum with fatigue, their brows furrowed with worry, hands buried deep within pockets or muffs.

The red bricks of the shops and smithies and tightly-packed houses are all blackened with filth. A train chugs noisily overhead and dark flakes descend from the overhanging bridge, mingling with the glistening snowflakes.

Down in the deep level, where I am employed, I constantly feel as if the walls are closing in on me. As if at any moment the weight of the world above may finally become too much for them, causing them to collapse upon me, crushing me with a million tonnes of earth and rock and clay and mud and houses and people. But strangely, today, I feel no different up here in the world above. The buildings all look to me to be too tall for their own foundations. They seem to lean in on me, threatening to collapse and engulf me at any moment.

I hurry onward with my prize in my breast pocket. I cannot resist every few seconds putting a hand there to make sure it has not been lost. Also, I cannot help but think that every time I do this someone notices and gives a nod to a partner-in-crime who proceeds to follow me until I venture into some dingy alley away from prying eyes. And yet I cannot stop doing it.

Soho Square Gardens provides a brief respite from the sense of claustrophobia. Then it's past St Patricks, right onto Sutton Row and I'm home. I am greeted by the comforting aroma of the oxtail soup that is gently bubbling away in a great, black pot on the iron stove. Bread is warming in the oven.

"Children," I hear a voice say. "Your father is home."

Squeals of delight are immediately followed by a stampede of little legs, and I am engulfed with hugs and festooned with kisses.

"Daddy! Daddy!" chirrups little George. "I did a painting of you! Come and see!" And I am dragged into the drawing room where I seat myself in the armchair next to the coal fire. The crackling embers breathe flickering life into the shadows, and all is good. My wife enters and places a glass of mulled wine on the small table next to me and plants a kiss

upon my forehead.

"Gather around, all," I say. "I have news."

"What news, daddy?" asks little Anne with relish. Although still young and naive in the workings of the world, she somehow senses the excitement that I am carrying with me, and allows it to possess her. She bounds over and places herself upon my knee.

"Daddy! Daddy!" George's hand is thrust straight up in the air. He desperately wants to ask something but...

"Sush, George." May, my beautiful wife, smiles. "Your father is speaking."

And so, in the cosy embrace of our glowing hearth and with my loving family gathered around, I impart my good news.

"Oh, my dearest ones," I begin. "Without whom I would be such a lesser man." I am relishing every word. "I arrive home today in even higher spirits than usual, if that were even possible."

My wife and children all chuckle and share loving glances.

"And why, I hear you ask. Quite simply, because of this..." and I pull from my breast pocket a sealed brown envelope and hold it aloft for all to acknowledge. "Within this small packet," I say, licking my lips, "is the sum of one hundred pounds."

Gasps all round.

"Which means that we are no longer in debt. It means brand new outfits for George and Anne, so that they may look their very best in school."

Squeals of delight.

"A beautiful new dress for my beautiful wife."

A sigh of pure love accompanied by a fluttering of the eyelashes.

"A brand-new suit for yours truly. And..."

I never reach the 'and' as I am once again engulfed with hugs and festooned with kisses.

"Oh, my darling Elias," swoons May. "Such a day! Such a day! But how did this wonderful thing come to be?"

And that, as they say, is the tricky part.

As previously stated, the above sadly never came to pass. Had it done so I can all but guarantee that there would have been a lot less hugging and considerably more fighting amongst the children. One of them would inevitably have ended up crying. May most certainly would not have been that pleased to greet me. She seldom was, being far too busy in the kitchen or trying to stop the children from killing each other.

It is a meticulously detailed reverie, is it not? But here's the thing: it probably lasted no more than a second when I originally experienced it. It is a frequent occurrence: a situation takes place and in but an instant a thousand possible outcomes flash through one's mind. It's as if every possible scenario presents itself, and the only work left for you to do is choose. Do I run away, or do I fight? Do I say no, or do I say yes?

I was presented with such a dilemma in my distant past, a stark yes or no choice. Although in this case, a full explanation of what answering in the affirmative would entail was not forthcoming. Had it been so, I most certainly would have declined. Needless to say, I did not realise at the time that I was making a life or death decision. Or that I would never again see daylight. Or that my wife and children would from that moment on exist merely as memories.

I knew him only as 'The Agent'. Not one of us toiling away down there in the deep level knew his real name. All we knew was that he was the go-between, the intermediary between "us" and "them". It was a condition of the job that we did not ask questions. It was also required of us to never speak of what we witnessed.

Since beginning my employ, I had seen things that had made me uncomfortable. All us engine drivers had. Oh, it had all started off respectfully enough. The bell would go and the telephone would be answered and the receptionist would come into the workshop and say, 'Mr so-and-so to be picked up from Westminster and taken to The Club', and whoever it was on duty would pop his cap on and step onto the footplate and do it. The engines were always kept stoked and ready and the carriages polished, for the calls could come at any time of the day or the night.

Our instructions had been clear, never speak to the clients, never make eye contact, never ask any questions. Just pick up and deliver. But over time the sights had grown stranger and the rumours wilder. Oh, there was a lot of talk amongst us drivers and engineers and operators. So-and-so had had to go and pick up some ladies and he reckoned they were prostitutes. And such-and-such had picked up some very queer looking young men who he reckoned were rent boys. And whatsisface had picked up a bunch of kids, real young 'uns, and taken them to The Quarters. It just doesn't bear thinking about.

And just when I thought things couldn't get any stranger, I was tasked with picking up a bunch of men wearing black cloaks and hoods. None of them said anything as they got on. They were all silent. And then I had to drop them off at The Library. So strange. And then Fred Barking said that he picked up some elderly gent with a long grey beard wearing all these brightly coloured robes and carrying a trident! Unfathomable!

Say what you want about debauchery, at least I can't get my head around it. At least I have some notion of what it is. But all this? I just couldn't figure it out. None of us could. It was madness. And Fred Barking said much the same after dropping a bunch of monks off at The Library. Later on, when he was going past again, he stopped outside and could hear all this strange chanting coming from within. Really gave him the willies, it did.

They say that discretion is the better part of valour, but to my good self, after a year spent working as an engine driver all the way down here in the deep level, it is nothing more than a monstrous burden. With every passing day my head fills up with yet more occurrences, disturbances and sights that I would wish to forget. But instead, I am required to carry them with me for the rest of my days without ever telling a soul.

So after all these peculiar comings and goings I could feel myself getting ever closer to my wits end, as you can imagine, and was genuinely thinking about jacking it all in. But then I was called into The Agent's office.

I have revisited the following event in my mind many times, as well I might what with it being so pivotal and all, and each time it is slightly different, so I would classify it as a reconstruction:

I rap on the door.

"Come!" shouts the voice from inside.

I enter. The flimsy walls do little to filter out the cacophony from the workshop beyond; the banging, the clanging, the coarse language. I have never been one for coarse language, myself.

"Ah, Mr Timms. Thank you for coming so promptly. Do sit down."

The Agent's manners are always impeccable, but he has a certain air about him that I find disconcerting. It is the air that a certain class of person always carries with him. How to explain? A certain class of person issues an order without even having the room in their mind to entertain the possibility that their order might not be obeyed instantly, and without question.

They issue orders and they are carried out. And that is that. When they ask questions, they are answered. When they want something, it is brought. Their comfort and convenience transcends all other considerations.

To them, class is everything. You might be the greatest painter who ever lived, but if you were born into a poor situation you are of no greater value to them than a mule. If you are destined to die penniless and starving then so be it, just make sure by doing it you do not impede their journey to dinner.

The Agent is such a man but, as I say, his manners are impeccable.

I sit and remove the driver's cap from my head.

"Mr Timms," he begins. "An opportunity has arisen. How

would you like to earn a hundred pounds?"

I stumble and mutter. How would I like to earn a hundred pounds? Did he really just ask that? I should like to earn a hundred pounds very much. What man wouldn't? And here I was toying with the idea of handing in my notice and finding myself a new situation up above in the sweet light of day. But there are reservations. The deep level has become a sinister place. Yes, that is the word for it: sinister. There is not a working man down here who has not had his view of the world considerably changed by the things he has seen and heard.

"Well?" asks The Agent.

I hate myself for ringing my cap in my hands, but I cannot help myself. It is a symptom of a lifetime spent in deference. A hundred pounds! Oh, why did such an offer have to come my way now, just as I am at the point of quitting. Temptation has a bad habit of always springing into your path at the most inopportune times.

But just think of what I could do with such a sun. It is at this point that the previously described reverie plays itself out in my mind's eye, and I make a resolution: I shall accept his offer, get my money and then quit. Yes, that is what I shall do. And so it is settled.

"Yes, sir," I finally say. "I accept your most generous offer. Thank you very much."

"Good. Good. I knew I could rely on you, Timms. A client hired a man to perform a task later today and that man has let us down. We require you to fill in for him."

"Doing what, sir?"

"All will be explained when you arrive, Timms."

"Arrive where, sir?"

"At The Club. Nine o'clock. Don't be late."

"Aye, sir."

"And I don't need to ask if I can rely on your discretion, do I?"

"Of course not, sir."

"Oh, and one more thing."

"Sir?"

135

"I am right in thinking that you are a Capricorn, am I not?"

"Aye, sir." And with this, I can't help but notice a bead of sweat trickle down The Agent's face.

Needless to say, events did not transpire quite the way I imagined they would, and that was the moment in which my fate was sealed.

But now I feel uneasy about what awaits me in that playground of immorality, and I have a pain in my guts. However, at the same time my head is spinning at the thought of going home to my wife and children with a hundred beautiful pounds in my hand.

What could the members of The Club possibly want me for? Do they just require an extra body to take coats? No, that would not warrant the offer of such a generous remuneration. What if they were in need of someone to join in with their acts of depravity? But then, why on earth would they choose me? None of this makes any sense. But then, what down here does?

All our lives we are taught to revere and respect the rich and powerful, to grovel in their presence, to walk in their shadows. To them we are invisible. To them we are not people with families and lives and aspirations and worth. We fall into two categories, nuisances and servants.

When my deep level days are over, I think, I will never look at a well-to-do man in his top hat and fur cape in the same way again. From now on, I will see monster in disguise. A filthy, degraded, depraved beast.

So, whatever horror it is that awaits me in The Club, I resolve to grit my teeth and endure it. Besides, I have already said yes to the offer and I pride myself on being a man of my word, so there is to be no backing out now.

The appointed time draws near, and Fred Barking has been kind enough to take me to The Club in one of the engines. How pleasant it is to be a passenger for a change.

Fred Barking is clearly feeling as uneasy as I about this whole affair.

"It's no place for the likes of us," he says as the engine noisily clanks and hisses its way through the tunnels. "That lot inhabit a different world to us, and I should prefer to steer well clear of them. However, needs must."

It was fifteen minutes to midnight and my feelings of uneasiness had mutated into convulsions of sickly dread. My palms were clammy and shaking and my throat dry. I was grateful for Fred's endless monologue. For as long as he was speaking, I did not need to.

"I'm telling you," he rambled on. "All the things that apply to us don't apply to the likes of them, like manners and good behaviour and faithfulness. We are obliged to face consequences for the heinous deeds we commit. For them, 'consequences' is just a word in the dictionary. If we behaved the way they do we'd be locked up. Locked up and disgraced and cast out from our families. We'd spend the rest of our lives living in shame. But them, they've no morals. None whatsoever. They can afford not to have with their money. They can behave however they like and there's no one to make them pay for it, and that's because the ones who are supposed to make them pay for it are also rich and hence writhing around in the same muck as this lot. They're all in it together."

By now I have stopped listening to the meaning of Fred's words and am simply marvelling at the sheer amount of them that are spilling out of his mouth. He is like a waterfall that never stops flowing.

"They're animals, the lot of them, giving in to their base desires without ever pausing to consider whether they should or not. They're at it all shapes with their tarts and their young boys and their talking to the dead and whatnot..."

Talking to the dead? My stomach curdles.

"...and still we have to tip our hats to them. It ain't right. It's them who should be tipping their hats to us. We're the superior ones. We're the ones with the good manners, who conduct ourselves like gentlemen. Right, here we are."

The engine screeches to a stop and I try to decide if I am relived or disappointed. After a moment's contemplation, I conclude that I would rather endure Fred's endless witterings for another hour than to spend ten minutes in The Club with the targets of his ire. That said, Fred's company does not come with the offer of a hundred pounds, and so I alight.

"Good luck," he says, and in I go.

What occurred within The Club will forever live in my mind as clear as crystal. The episode requires no reconstruction. However, even to this day I struggle to confront it.

Immediately upon entering, a black hood is placed over my head. However, in the instant prior to my hooding, I observe a great many fellows within, one in brightly coloured robes and the rest adorned entirely in black.

Faster than I can think, I am taken by the arms, laid flat onto a table and binds secured around my wrists and ankles. And that's when the chanting begins. At this point in time, I know not what my fate will be, but I have begun to fear the worst, and so I decide that my life is worth far more than hundred pounds and begin to scream and struggle as the chanting continues. It was my good fortune to be born fairly scrawny, and so I am able to slip my right hand through the binding and rip from my head the hood. The first thing I see is a golden dagger being held aloft by the man in the colourful robes. He is poised, I can tell, to plunge it into my heart. At this I discover a strength I have never known, not even during my toils as a fireman, and I rip the binding holding my right leg and kick out at him. He falls backward and I quickly free myself and make a run for it, pursued by the men in the black robes.

I exit The Club and find myself back on its platform. To my great surprise I see that Fred is still there, standing on his footplate idly smoking a cigarette. I know that there is no time for him to fire up his boiler and steer me to safety and so I run past him. He looks stunned, and understandably so. I leap down onto the tracks and flee into the tunnel.

And then, from behind me, I hear a voice. It is directed at Fred. "A hundred pounds if you apprehend that man," it says.

His reply is the single most horrific thing that ever reached my ears. "Aye, sir," he says, and then brings his engine to life.

I was pursued through the tunnels by that hissing and screeching engine and eventually caught. Fred, after everything he had said, betrayed me! He cowed in the presence of those immoral pigs and sacrificed his friend for a few notes in his hand. I was carried flailing and screaming back to The Club where I was once again hooded and bound. This time the ritual was completed.

To this day I cannot bear the shrieking of a steam engine. It is something that tortures me, torments me, and I will not countenance it.

But enough memories for one day. The mind, as I say, is a curious article, and I sincerely hope that all that I have recounted for you will help you to better understand that I was once as you are now, and wish I was still.

Chapter Eight

Rosalind began to laugh. And in the space of about a second-and-a-half, that laughter became hysterical. She couldn't believe that all her life-decisions had led to this, an horrific death at the hands of a demonic tunnel dweller deep underground ina forgotten Victorian labyrinth. The words 'Monster Munch' had opened the emotional floodgates, and it was hysteria that had gushed forth. It was simply the sheer, utter ridiculousness of it all.

And now her eyes were closed, and her head was back, and she was roaring with laughter. "Fucking Monster Munch!" she bellowed in her mania. "My favourite crisp! Those two words should be on my fucking gravestone! What an epitaph!"

The beast that had ensnared her by sucking out her life-force completely vanished from her mind. She didn't care now that she was going to die. It didn't matter. Go ahead! Kill me! Big fucking deal! Ha ha ha!

She opened her eyes, now red and streaked with tears of laughter. The tunnel dweller was still there, but it seemed to be fading back into the darkness. Dissolving, almost. Her mania began to subside, and she became aware that the force that had been feeding from her was losing its grip. A weight was lifting. The laughter subsided and left her panting for breath. She was no longer afraid. The creature had gone.

Still shuddering from exhaustion, she staggered to her feet. "I'm not afraid of you, anymore," she cackled. "You don't scare me, you ugly BASTARD!" This last word she delivered with real venom, straight from the pit of her soul. "Fuck off back to hell! I'm going home!"

In defiance, she turned her back on the platform and the

tunnel dweller and the silent engine and all the horrors that had occurred this day and proceeded to limp up the steps. And then her foot hit something, something that clattered noisily as it skipped across the floor and down a step or two. Rosalind picked it out in the flickering light of her head torch. It was a video camera, Rich's video camera! She picked it up and studied it for a moment, and then opened the other large pocket on the front of her coat, the one without a book in it, and slipped it inside.

First, Syd had given her something, and now Rich had too. But what about Fee? She couldn't leave without taking something of Fee's with her. Something that she could pass on to her loved ones. Once this thought had presented itself, Rosalind couldn't let it go. It had taken a hold inside her. She had to have something of Ffion's to take with her to the surface, so that at least a part of her would make it out. She swept her flickering beam of light up and down the steps. It rested on the pile of dust and cobwebs on the ground, and she realised then that nothing remained of her friend for her to take.

She did not know it, of course, but she already had something of Ffion's in her pocket, contained within Rich's camera, her final goodbyes. It was the most precious thing she could have found.

Inside Rosalind, a well began to fill up. It was gushing up towards the surface and there was no way she could stop it. The tears came in waves, convulsing her body with big, heavy sobs. She cried deeply and completely, purging herself of the terrible grief that had overcome her. And as she sobbed and wailed, the tunnel dweller began to gather its strength.

Even through the spasms of her sorrow, Rosalind could detect that something in the atmosphere had changed. She sensed the tiny, grey hairs on the back of her neck standing to attention, and so she choked back her tears and held her breath. A ripple of static electricity danced down her spine. Her eyes widened and her whole being stiffened as she sensed a presence approaching from behind. If she was ever going to run, the time was now, and so she did.

141

The tunnel dweller fed on fear and weakness and dread. Those were the chinks in a person's armour that allowed it in. And once in it would suck out the life force of a being in the same way that a spider drained the innards of a fly. But conversely, this meant that it could be beaten. If one could hold ones fear in check, suppress the primal instinct to surrender reason to panic, then it could be outwitted, outran, but it would take every reserve of strength, anger and defiance that Rosalind had. However, she had the will now to fight, to escape and to survive. Not just for herself and her husband and her children, but also for her fallen friends; for Syd and Fee and Rich. She had to live for them. She had to make it to the surface so that a piece of them could live through her. So that their stories could be told.

She felt as if she were made of iron. With jaw and fists clenched, she soldiered forward; left at the top of the stairs, follow the passageway around and then left again. But everything looked different in the flickering light of her head torch. Had she come the wrong way? She did not know and there was no way for her to find out. No clues, no points of reference, just identical tunnels and entrances and stairways. Her ears popped as the air thickened. It was closing in on her again. An aged greyness fell over her eyes and her focus began to wane. She felt her spirit start to seep away as her legs turned to jelly and her muscles softened. But she knew now how to break the creature's hold. All she had to do was shout and scream and yell.

"YOU WILL NOT TAKE ME!" she roared. "YOU WILL NOT TAKE ME, YOU BASTARD! YOU CAN'T HAVE ME!"

She clawed the cobwebs from her eyes and hauled herself upright and pushed her weary body on. But it was hard, so very hard. She could feel the greyness upon her again, but she cast it off and refused to succumb.

"LEAVE ME ALONE YOU EVIL FUCKING BASTARD!" she screamed. The screaming and yelling fuelled her anger and reinforced hersense of defiance. Her voice was the well from which her strength sprang.

It's right up ahead, she thought. I'm sure of it. *That's the way out of here.* Empowered by hope and the promise of deliverance, her body was suddenly revitalised. Her spine straightened and she felt lightening-like bursts of power in her leg muscles. She ran on. *That cross*, she thought. *Those names around the cross. It's a seal. It's what keeps that thing trapped down here. It can't pass it. It can't get me if I...if I...*

By her nature Rosalind was a thinker. Her mind was inclined to examine, to search for patterns and meanings and reasons, even if there were none to be found. And it was this unquiet mind of hers that, at the moment of her salvation, left her exposed. As the voice in her head had risen, so her raw, primal will to survive had subsided.

"No," she gasped feebly as she realised too late the mistake that she had made. Her intellect had let the tunnel dweller in, and now the cold, grey nothingness had her. In an instant, every ounce of strength that she had found drained from her and, weak and limp, her body collapsed onto the wet, hard ground.

As her flesh, blood and bone surrendered to the dust and her vision receded into a grey fog, Rosalind, silently, despaired at the cruelty of it all; the fact that her end should come with safety within such tantalising reach. She had fallen just an arms-length away from the threshold. The threshold that, earlier that same day, she and her friends had uncovered behind the brick wall. The threshold that bore the seal. The threshold over which the tunnel dweller could not cross.

Summoning up her final reserve of strength, as a coven might summon up a demon, she reached forward, grasping at the freedom that lay just beyond the doorway. And then she felt something wrap itself around the wrist of her outstretched arm, something cold and clammy like long, bony fingers. Inside her cocoon a spark flashed across her brain. There was still a tiny concentration of consciousness there. *It's got me*, it thought. *It's got me. It's over.*

There was a sudden lurch and her body was dragged forward. Then there was a bump. What was that? Had she crossed the threshold? And now she was being dragged to her feet. She could move again. With her free hand she pawed at her face, pulling the dust and cobwebs away. But still all was black. Her head torch, she realised, had finally died. But something was still clutching her by the wrist. What was it?

She tried to speak. Her mouth moved but no words emerged. And then she became aware of a smell. She *knew* that smell! She had experienced it before. It was the sickly-warm stench of human faeces and urine. Was this the person who lived in the train carriage? The person who had thrown the stone at her and her friends?

Confused, disorientated and voiceless, Rosalind felt her body being pulled forward by the wrist. Her legs, still jelly-like, automatically followed. She was being led away from the horror that was still prowling somewhere behind her, just beyond the threshold.

Oh, thank god! Thank god!

Something caught her eye. A flicker of light. A pinpoint of warmth in a cold sea of blackness. It was a lone candle, illuminating the interior of the abandoned train carriage that Rosalind and her friends had been peering into earlier.

So someone does live down here! said the voice inside her head. The voice outside her head, conversely, was still not cooperating. Her guide also said nothing. And so, with an unspoken understanding between them, Rosalind was led silently back to the world above.

She knew she was back at surface level when she started hearing birds flapping somewhere above her. And then she noticed pinpricks of light cutting through tiny gaps in the walls. Her ears detected a noise; the familiar hum of London traffic, the ever-present background static of continuing life. As they walked on it became louder and louder, and eventually she could make out individual sounds; cars, horns, people, a baby crying. She realised then that all that stood between her and the outside world was a brick wall – such a fragile thing –and a tidal wave of emotion swept over her. Her body and mind began to purge, and tears gushed from her eyes.

Her wrist was released, and her mysterious guide melted away into the shadows. And then Rosalind finally found her voice.

"Thank you," she whispered. "Thank you so very, very much." And finally, "Be safe."

She was in a vast, cavernous space, but not the same cavernous space that her terrible adventure had commenced in. This one was not so old, so ruined. It was the remains of an old train station. There were benches, turnstiles, tiled floors, posters on the walls, a ticket office; but everything was still covered in a thick layer of dust and bird shit.

Light was finding its way in through the edges of the doors on the far side of the empty hall. As pigeons cooed above her, she staggered forward in a semi-daze. As she approached, the sounds from without grew louder, and the louder they grew the faster Rosalind moved. She was now half-running, half-limping.

As she reached the doors her primal survival instinct returned with a vengeance and she began pulling and clawing at them, but they would not give. There was sunlight and people and life just beyond them, mere feet away, but completely out of her reach, like a nightmare.

And then the levees broke and she began smashing her fists against the doors and screaming: "HEEEELP! HEEEELP! GET ME OUT OF HERE! FOR FUCK'S SAKE GET ME OUT OF HERE! HEEEELP! HEEELP!"

Outside, people began to gather. There's someone trapped in there! Are you alright, love? Try the doors. No, it's no good. We'll have to call the police or something. Jesus, love, calm down! What's happening?

"FOR FUCK'S SAKE GET ME OUT! HEEELP! HEEELP!"

And unbeknownst to Rosalind, at that precise moment, her husband and sons and mother-in-law and friend were all just a few miles away, sitting around a coffee table playing Trivial Pursuit and waiting for her to come home.

Chapter Nine

"Morning, ladies," said a familiar voice. "Are we all ready?"

"You can wait till I've finished my sodding breakfast first, Rich," said Ffion.

"Hey, Rich. How's it going?" asked Syeeda, whilst taking a sip from her mug of coffee. Black, as Jason had yet to discover soya milk.

"Crap," replied Rich, deadpan as always.

"Are you having any breakfast?" Ffion asked, ignoring his negativity. "Roz's paying."

"Oi!" Rosalind exclaimed.

"In that case I'll have a sausage sandwich and a cuppa." He turned towards Jason who was standing upright and stiff in his steamed-up glasses behind the counter. "Sausage sandwich and a cuppa please, Jase."

"ALRIGHT, BOY! COMING UP!"

Rich took a seat. "Cheers, Roz."

"That's alright," sighed Rosalind, aiming a glare at Ffion.

Ffion, completely oblivious to Rosalind's burning eyes, said, "Oi, Rich. Syeeda wants to know what kind of crisp you are."

"What kind of crisp I am?"

"Yeah," said Syeeda. "If you were a crisp, what kind of crisp would you be?"

"Where's this come from?"

"Work," Syeeda lied. In truth she had stumbled upon this in a marketing book, one that Alan the interviewer had recommended to her when he had called to tell her she had got the job. It was a quirky way to make company bosses think creatively about their businesses. It was all part of the prep for when she started. She knew that this was Her Big

Break and she didn't want to blow it.

"But I don't even like crisps."

"Well, that doesn't matter. I'm not after which crisp is your favourite, just which kind of crisp do you think best represents you."

Rich thought for a moment. "Crisps really aren't my field of expertise, but I can tell you what kind of biscuit I'd be."

"Go on then."

"A digestive."

"Why a digestive?"

"Because there's absolutely nothing fancy about it whatsoever. In fact, even the name is literal. Digestive. It's named after what happens to it once you've eaten it."

Ffion grimaced. "You've just put me off digestives for life."

Syeeda's eyes lit up. "So if you apply that logic to crisps, you'd be a plain old ready salted crisp, with nothing fancy about it whatsoever."

"Yes, I suppose I would be."

"I think you're selling yourself a bit short there, Rich," said Rosalind. "I don't think you're plain and unremarkable."

"Same," said Syeeda.

"All we need now is for Roz to tell us what kind of crisp she'd be," Ffion said to Rich. "She can't decide."

"I just don't see why it's so important." Roz shrugged.

Jason placed a sausage sandwich and a cup of tea in front of Rich. "HERE YOU GO, FELLA!"

"Thanks, Jase. You're a pal."

"NO PROBLEM! ENJOY!"

"We've been swapping funny stories from work," said Ffion to Rich with a smile. "You got any?"

"I have, actually," Rich replied, arching an eyebrow. "I had a customer in the bookshop earlier this week – elderly fella – and he comes up to me and he says, 'I'm looking for a book for my grandson. I wonder if you can help me'. So I say, 'Okay. What are you looking for?' And he says, 'It's not one I'm familiar with myself, so I'm not sure if you'll have it in stock. It's for my grandson. He sent me in for it.' He keeps

147

saying it's for his grandson. And then he pulls a piece of paper from his pocket and starts unfolding it. 'As I say,' he says, 'it's not one I'm familiar with, but I said I'd ask.' And then he looks at this piece of paper, stares at it really intently for a few seconds, and then he looks at me all apologetically and he says, 'Lord of the Rings?'"

The whole table erupted into laughter.

"Aw, bless," Ffion gushed.

"That's so cute," whimpered Syeeda.

"Honestly," said Rich. "You couldn't make it up."

"So, Rich," said Rosalind, changing the subject, "is this going to be a one-off adventure, or is it going to be a regular occurrence?"

The laughter abated and all eyes turned to Rich.

"Well, if it all goes well today, maybe we will do this regularly."

Everyone was very obviously pleased with this answer.

"Brilliant," exclaimed Ffion. "We'll have to think of a name for ourselves. Like a team name."

"How about the Urbex-Men?" Rich suggested.

"I don't get it," said Syeeda.

"Urbex is the abbreviation of urban explorer. Urban explorers refer to themselves as urbexes. So, you know, Urbex-Men. Like the X-Men."

"Never mind the fact that three out of the four of us are women," Rosalind pointed out.

"Yeah, well, there is that," Rich conceded.

"If only the Fantastic Four didn't exist," said Ffion. "That would be an awesome name."

"Come on, Syd," said Rosalind. "You're supposed to be the creative one. Can't you think of something?"

Syeeda screwed up her face for a moment, thinking hard. "Okay, how about...The Exploresome Foursome?"

Everyone laughed with delight.

"Ha ha! I love it!" squealed Ffion.

"Brilliant!" exclaimed Rich, slapping his hand down onto the table.

Behind the counter, Jason was craning his neck, trying to

discern what all the jollity was about.

"How *do* you come up with this stuff?" Rosalind asked.

Syeeda, basking in the praise of her friends, sank back into her chair with a satisfied smile on her face.

"I tell you what, Syd," grinned Ffion, "you should write about our adventures."

"Now that's a good idea," agreed Rosalind. "What do you think, Rich?"

Rich nodded. "Yeah. I'd read that," he said.

For a fleeting, golden moment, Syeeda considered sharing with her friends the exciting news about her new job, about the fact that she was actually going to be a professional writer. But then, she decided to hang onto it for just a little bit longer. Perhaps she would tell them later, when they emerged blinking and triumphant into the sunlight following the day's explorations.

"Right then," said Rich, polishing off his (second) breakfast and looking at his watch. "I think we'd better be off."

"Before we do," said Rosalind, "how about a toast?" She raised her coffee mug. "To The Exploresome Foursome!"

"The Exploresome Foursome!" they all repeated, clinking their mugs together.

And then they left to spend their last ever day together, exploring the forgotten underground tunnels of London, somewhere down in the deep level.

THE END

Fantastic Books
Great Authors

darkstroke is
an imprint of
Crooked Cat Books

- Gripping Thrillers
- Cosy Mysteries
- Romantic Chick-Lit
- Fascinating Historicals
- Exciting Fantasy
- Young Adult
- Non-Fiction

Discover us online
www.darkstroke.com

Find us on instagram:
www.instagram.com/darkstrokebooks

Printed in Great Britain
by Amazon